The Cookie Match

MAPLE GARDENS MATCHMAKERS 4

PHILLIPA NEFRI CLARK

Copyright © The Cookie Match by Phillipa Nefri Clark

All rights reserved.

No part of this publication may be reproduced, distributed, or transmitted in any form or by any means, including photocopying, recording, or other electronic or mechanical methods, without the prior written permission of the publisher, except as permitted by U.S. copyright law. For permission requests, contact hello@phillipaclark.com.

The story, all names, characters, and incidents portrayed in this production are fictitious. No identification with actual persons (living or deceased), places, buildings, and products is intended or should be inferred.

Book Cover by Wynter Designs

Editing by DP Plus

The Cookie Match

Chapter One

Maximus Stone charged out of the Maple Gardens main building like his pants were on fire. One more year down. One more family day in the books. Three years he'd been doing this. And for three years he'd hated every last minute of it.

At least one good thing had come from attending this year. He'd finally been able to meet Peter, the man behind the delectable meals at Maple Gardens.

The buzz surrounding the retirement community had ticked up in recent months thanks to Quinne Hart, a social media influencer who seemed to have a knack in the kitchen and had her own family connection to the assisted living complex. Max wasn't the only one who had noticed either. Especially when Quinne started an online cooking series featuring some of the residents. His own mother even got the spotlight in one of the segments.

Max trudged toward his sports car, fully aware of the strange looks he received on his way out. Family day wasn't technically over yet. There were still activities going on and several visitors were still arriving.

Two hours. That was how much time he'd promised Lily Stone. His mother.

But he hadn't viewed her as such for at least ten years. When he was a teenager she'd made decisions which had changed his life. Most were detrimental. He'd lost his dearest friend and, and yet to this day she didn't seem to take any responsibility for it.

He rested his hands on the steering wheel and stared hard at nothing in particular. His hands tightened then relaxed as he focused on his breathing.

Every single person he knew had told him that this grudge he held was unhealthy. The thing was, he knew that. And yet there was nothing he could do to stop it. There was this barrier inside him that prevented him from letting go of the betrayal he'd endured.

What kind of mother kept her son from his father for his entire life, only to admit the truth shortly after the man died?

No mother of his.

Max's jaw tightened and a sharp pain emanated from where he clenched a bit too tight. Great. Next person who'd lecture him would be his dentist. He worked his jaw back and forth to relax the muscles there, but the ache remained.

There were more important matters to attend to. With Peter on board to cater Max's upcoming charity venture, there were only a few more things to finalize before he could put his rubber stamp of approval on the gala and send all the details to his event planner.

This year was going to be the biggest auction yet and, as always, the money raised would go toward several programs benefiting orphans and children in foster care. This time he'd added something new to the list. There was a set amount put aside to aid in children being reunited with parents that had been missing from their lives.

His thoughts cycled through the day he'd found out his

father hadn't actually died in an accident, as he'd been told. A man he didn't recognize came to the door and handed his mother a yellow folder. The man, a lawyer, informed Lily that Maximus Arnold Irving had passed away and left her a great deal of money. Seventeen years of watching other boys play catch with their fathers, of hearing stories about camping or fishing trips, and he suddenly found out there was no reason he should have missed out on all of that. All he had of his father was half of the inheritance, which his mother gave to him, with the promise of leaving him the rest in her will. As much as he hadn't wanted to be beholden to her, of course he took the money—it was the only part of his father he would ever have.

Max scowled, shoving the memory aside. He put the car into reverse, backed out of his parking spot then drove away from the place his mother now called home. Every time he came here, his sour mood returned.

There was only one way to drag himself out of this funk and that was to dive headfirst into work again. He needed the distraction—craved it. Thankfully, being the head of a tech company offered a lot of ways for him to lose himself in his work. He headed toward the busier part of the city. His building was the second tallest, and easy to see from most anywhere.

After graduating from MIT, he'd made sure to make something of himself. The inheritance from his father had helped to make that happen, so to show his appreciation, he named the business after the one person he wished he could have met.

Max drove up in front of a building lined with glass. The name, front and center in bold lettering, read *Maximus Irving Technologies*. Max might not have been given his father's last name, but one thing had been made clear by the generosity of the inheritance—his father had held his mother in his memory all those years, and no doubt would have been a loving father to Max. His father had lost just as much as he had by not knowing he had a son. That thought was the basis of his company.

He climbed out of his car and the young man behind the valet stand hurried toward him. "Good morning, Mr. Stone."

"Morning, Joseph. How are your folks doing?"

"Great. How's your mom?"

Max's throat tightened. It wasn't a secret his mother resided at Maple Gardens. She had been lonely after retiring as a teacher and decided to move to Maple Gardens so she could age on her own terms. Family day was a big deal and those who worked for him knew what to expect when the date arrived.

However, very few understood the exhaustion that came from pretending everything was okay. Max forced a smile at the young man as he patted his shoulder. "She's doing good. Thanks for asking."

Max headed inside through the nine-foot-high glass doors and nodded toward the security guard. Bud had to be nearing retirement age, and it showed. His grey hair and lined face demonstrated just how much of his life he'd lived. He waved a gnarled hand toward Max.

"Good morning, Mr. Stone."

"Morning."

"How's your mother?"

Max stiffened. "Same as always."

"So good of you to pay her a visit."

Once again, Max found himself with a smile plastered to his face that he didn't feel like wearing. He should be grateful that the people who worked for him took an interest in his life. He just wished they'd keep his so-called family out of it.

Max hurried toward the elevator if only to escape the sharp gaze of the man who had worked for him since he'd

THE COOKIE MATCH

bought this building. Thankfully there weren't any meetings today, so he could focus all his energy on the upcoming charity event.

Caterer, check.

Businesses to auction their goods or services, check.

Venue, check.

He exited the elevator and strode through the main lobby of the floor where his office was located. Cathy sat behind her desk and rose immediately when he arrived. She grabbed a clipboard, following him into his office as she started her speech.

"Bartholomew Brown called while you were out. He said he was hoping to catch you at family day, but since he missed you, he'd like to set up a time when you two can do lunch."

Max glanced at his secretary. "Did he say anything about why?" He picked up a stack of papers that had been placed on his desk and started to leaf through them as he glanced once more toward Cathy.

She shook her head. "Isaac Spencer also left a message around the same time. He wants to meet with you about the possibility of doing a joint event that will bring together foster children and those who live at Maple Gardens."

He looked up from the paper in his hand, considering what she'd said. "That's not a half-bad idea. The local kids around here could use some extra guidance and the Kids Club is overrun with children who are in the program already. We could make it a kind of meeting of the generations matchmaking venture." He pulled out his desk chair and opened a blank document on his computer. "We could give the kids and the adults a questionnaire that would help them find people with similar interests."

When he met Cathy's gaze, he wasn't surprised to find her grinning at him. Her dark eyes shone a little brighter at his glance. She reached up and tucked a strand of wavy dark hair behind her ear. "I think that sounds wonderful. I can call around and see who might be willing to sponsor something like that."

He shook his head. "We're doing this one all on our own. In fact, I think I'll call a few of my business partners and see if they're interested in starting a non-profit that will bring this to fruition sooner." Max typed vigorously at his computer as he made notes on what this program could accomplish. Once he got it off the ground, they'd contact companies who were interested in helping.

"Kirsten called, too."

His head popped up, noting immediately how Cathy's expression had shifted to something neutral, though it bordered on disgust. Max bit back a smile. "What did Miss Lane want?"

"She wanted to know if you have finalized everything for this next charity event. She wants to start ordering what she'll need and wanted me to emphasize that you need to give her a head count."

"Kirsten has been doing this long enough to know that I don't have that sort of information yet. She's just going to have to wait until I reach out to a few more people."

"That's what I told her." Cathy's voice seemed to shift from guarded to proud, which caused him to glance at her again.

He wasn't oblivious. Since day one, Cathy had been somewhat overt about the fact she was interested in him. She hadn't officially asked him out, but there were signs. Depending on the client he was meeting with, her mood would shift. If it was an attractive woman, she had a tendency to show a little less cordiality. If it was a man, she was the perfect example of how a secretary should behave. She was a nice woman, but he'd opted to remain professional because nothing good ever came from dating someone one worked with. Max returned his focus to the computer. "Was that all of my messages?"

She didn't say anything right away, but then her voice softened. "Have you decided who you're going to ask to accompany you to the gala?"

Without glancing toward her, he shook his head. "I'll probably go alone, like I always do."

"Right. Of course." She shifted, and for a moment he thought she might say something else. But she didn't. Instead, she slipped out of his office. Only when her steps faded, did he glance in her direction again.

Besides his opinion on office romances being a terrible idea, he just wasn't that interested in long-term relationships. He hadn't really wanted to after discovering the secret his mother had kept from his father. Was it any wonder he had trouble trusting women?

"If you don't have an appointment, then you can't go in there." Cathy's firm voice penetrated into his office and his head snapped up. Whoever it was that thought they could just waltz in here and see him was out of their depth.

"Like I said, I don't have an appointment because I'm just delivering coffee." A woman's voice filtered through his office doors.

That voice was so familiar. Max couldn't place where he'd heard it before, but it tickled a memory in the back of his mind.

"We have an excellent coffee machine. There is no way that we ordered anything from your little coffee shop."

"I'm sorry. But they are already paid for and I'm not going anywhere until they're delivered. A missing delivery isn't worth losing my job over."

Max launched from his chair and rounded his desk.

It couldn't be. That voice, there was no way ...

He made it to his doorway slowly enough not to draw her

attention. She looked just as he remembered her. Blonde hair and blue-green eyes. A snub nose and a splash of freckles across its bridge. Max hadn't seen Ava since they were in high school, but he would recognize her anywhere.

She must have felt his eyes on her, because, even though he didn't move, she turned her head in his direction. Cathy did too, her face flushed with annoyance.

Max's eyes locked with Ava's and it was like a hook had stabbed into his heart and dragged him back in time to when he was seventeen.

Chapter Two

There had only ever been one Maximus Stone.

Ava hadn't wanted to take this delivery, for the very reason that she knew in her soul this wouldn't turn out the way she wanted it to. She should have just left the coffee with his annoying secretary. Then at least she wouldn't have to come face to face with the one man she had wondered about since he'd left for another school all those years ago.

And at the same time, she couldn't deny the way just seeing him filled her with the utmost joy. Her happiness outweighed the nerves, and she placed a hand on her hip as she tilted her head slightly. "Maximus Stone, as I live and breathe."

"Ava." His voice was noticeably lower than when she'd last seen him. Then again, it had been a decade. She gestured toward the drink tray with two coffees in it. "I got an online order to bring this to you. But apparently you're too good for the old-fashioned stuff. Let me guess. You're into espressos from those little pod machines."

The smile she had hoped to see appeared on his face but this one was different. It didn't reach his dark brown eyes, so there was no adorable crinkling around them. He'd grown a short beard, which made him appear older and more distinguished. A slight flutter in her chest reminded her that she was in fact female, and just looking at him set off a chain reaction of goose bumps and chills.

Max's attention shifted momentarily to his secretary, then back to Ava. "Go ahead and let her in. She's an old friend."

Without looking toward his secretary, Ava scooped up the coffees and headed toward Max. Never in a million years had she thought she'd see him again. Not face to face. After all, he was living life in a whole different world from the one they used to inhabit.

Max didn't move when she approached, instead he nodded toward his office and let her go inside first.

There were so many unspoken words between them. Too many life experiences they hadn't shared.

Who was she kidding? They weren't friends. Time had made them strangers. She knew this Maximus Stone no better than any guy she might have passed on the street.

A small ache started low in her stomach and grew steadily as she made her way to the desk and put the tray of coffees there. Her gaze swept through the room, taking in everything that showcased who the new Max was.

Windows stretched from floor to ceiling on one side of the room, showing off the view of the city. On either side of that glass wall, built-in bookshelves were practically bursting with various volumes. Her legs seemed to have a mind of their own as she wandered to the right. This bookshelf was clearly reserved for literature rather than the kinds of technical books a guy like Max would use in his business dealings.

Ava's fingertip traced along the wooden shelf with reverence as she noted the titles of several classics they'd been forced to read in high school. She glanced over her shoulder, finding Max had shut the door and leaned against it. His eyes had probably followed her from the moment she entered the room and she didn't know whether or not she liked that idea.

A smile tugged at her lips as she jerked her chin toward the bookshelf. "I thought you hated English. That's why you got into tech stuff, wasn't it?"

He lifted a brow. "Sounds like you've been reading up on me."

She felt the warmth creep across her skin and flood her cheeks. "To be fair, you sorta became this big local celebrity and since I wasn't good enough to remain your friend—"

Max pushed away from the door and moved toward her. "What makes you say that?"

"Say what?"

"That you're not good enough to be my friend?"

Her blush intensified. "Well, after you moved you didn't exactly keep in touch for long. Just one call with the phone number at your new house." Ava tore her gaze away from him, turning toward the bookcase again, and drew in a deep breath before attempting to release it without being noticed. "I'm guessing it got harder to maintain a friendship with someone like me when you're busy trying to fit into a new world."

"You're wrong."

His voice was directly behind her. She could practically feel the warmth of his body coming off him in waves. It pulsated like a heartbeat, warm and sure. Unfortunately, it was the sort of thing that sent fierce shivers down her spine. Ava didn't dare turn around. She knew this conversation was inevitable. The way they'd left things was enough to put a strain on any relationship—especially a friendship like they'd had.

"Do you really believe that?" he murmured.

If she turned to face him, the bookshelves would dig into her back and she already felt cornered enough. Ava shifted, moving away from where Max stood and headed for the window. She shrugged, her voice barely above a whisper. "You were my best friend, Max. How else would I interpret the way things changed?" This time she faced him. Thankfully he remained by the bookshelves. Only now, he had rested his elbow on a shelf and he was staring out the window with a pensive look on his face.

And such a handsome face. It had her wondering why he wasn't dating anyone.

Okay, he probably *was* dating someone and was willing to pay a premium to keep that sort of information out of the public eye. Once again her thoughts betrayed her and the flush that flooded her features gave her away. Hopefully he hadn't noticed just how embarrassing this conversation had become.

"The door swings both ways, Ava."

She stilled, then dragged her focus to meet his gaze.

"I know I wasn't the best at keeping in touch with you. But I don't think I remember getting a single phone call from you."

"I tried."

His brows pulled together sharply.

Ava nodded. "I called you several times. Left messages, too. But when you didn't return any of them, I figured you had moved on." Her stomach swirled at the memory. It had been the most heartbreaking moment in her entire life. For a long time she had thought she'd overreacted, but in time she'd realized her feelings were warranted. It just took a while to come to terms with them and move on.

Max's expression continued to tighten as her words seemed to sink in with each passing moment. "You did?"

Ava nodded. "Of course I did. At first, I thought you needed time to settle in. But then later, I realized ..." She swallowed hard. "I just figured you had moved on."

He took a sudden step toward her, then stopped short. "I never got anything from you." His eyes dropped to the ground. "I can only think of one reason ..." His focus shifted once more to her. "I don't know what happened, but this wasn't either of our faults."

She wasn't sure, but she could have sworn she saw anger flicker behind his eyes—it was almost fury. Ava forced a smile, the small amount of relief she experienced overshadowed by the disappointment of how much time she'd lost that she could have spent with him. "It's okay. We just ended up going our separate ways, like we were meant to." Gesturing to his office, she gave him a teasing look. "Seems to me you turned out just fine."

When they had been younger, she would have never predicted just how separate their paths would end up being. There were several people who had insisted that she would end up with Max just because they were so close.

Had she wondered about that possibility over the years? Sure—especially when she'd see updates about him in the news. But she still had her grandmother and friends and a job she loved. There was a lot she was grateful for.

That look in Max's eyes remained, hovering just beneath the surface. It seemed to writhe there, seeking a way to escape. Ava tilted her head, her smile fading somewhat. "Is everything okay?"

He blinked and the anger was replaced by a flat mask. He rubbed his eyes with his fingers and thumb then nodded and met her gaze again. "You know that everything they put in the papers isn't true, right?"

She squinted at him. "So, you're not the billionaire who has single-handedly provided a means to help orphans and children in foster care find forever homes?" It took every ounce of self-restraint she had to hold back the laugh that threatened to burst from her lips. "That's a shame."

Max rolled his eyes. "Yeah, they kinda embellish things." He edged closer to her, stopping when he was at her side but still far enough away that she wouldn't have been able to touch him if she held her arm out toward him. Max stared out the window, his hands clasped behind his back. "I do what I can." His soft words set off a wave of goose bumps on her arms.

Watching him out of the corner of her eye, Ava couldn't help but notice he didn't seem all that happy. Money and fame didn't seem to suit him as much as she'd thought they would. Max actually looked unhappy—a shell of the person she knew when she was in high school.

She scooted closer to him, keeping her eyes trained on the view as she murmured, "You're doing more than anyone would ever expect from you."

He gave her a side-eyed look. "There's always more I could be doing. Like you said ... I've made out better than I could have dreamed when we were younger."

Ava was now close enough she could nudge him with her elbow. "Don't be so modest. You're doing incredible things. Anyone with eyes can see it." She noticed a ghost of a smile grace his lips and a faint thrill rippled through her.

Memories of their friendship had continued to trickle to the forefront of her mind and all it had taken was that one smile for the floodgates to release all of them.

Oh, how she yearned to return to simpler times when it was just the two of them sitting beneath the bleachers, laughing about something or reading together. Her gaze drifted once more to the bookshelf and she noticed something she hadn't before. There on the edge of one of the shelves was a copy of *Pygmalion*. A fresh wave of goose bumps lifted on her arms as her eyes locked on the book.

That was the last one she'd forced him to read. He'd insisted he didn't need to read it because he could just watch the movie *My Fair Lady* and get the gist of the story. She remembered the conversation like it was yesterday.

It had been the last day she'd seen him, because he moved the next day.

Feeling his gaze on her, she swiveled her face toward him. His eyes studied her as if he were calculating something in his head. Neither one of them moved at first, both frozen in time. When he finally opened his mouth, she cut him off.

"Well, I better get back. I've taken far too long with this delivery. I'm sure they're going to cut my pay and I can't have that." She winked at him. "It's not like I have a million dollars." She shoved her hands into her apron and spun around to head for the door.

"Ava, wait."

Chapter Three

Max hurried after Ava, relieved when she paused to face him with her hand on the door. She met his eyes, but it didn't appear that she was thrilled about doing so. "Could we ... Would you like to get a coffee with me?"

At first she just stared at him blankly. He might have thought she hadn't heard him, but then she snickered as she motioned toward the drinks he had on his desk. "I just brought you the drinks you ordered."

He glanced over his shoulder toward the coffees then back to her, shaking his head. "I didn't, actually, but that doesn't matter. It's been ... nice ... catching up." More than nice. Seeing her again had reminded him more fully of his roots—where he'd come from before his mother had made the unilateral decision to use the inheritance from his father and cart him off somewhere far away from Ava. "Or we could get dinner."

Ava paled.

No, that was just his imagination. Her features tightened with what could only be described as discomfort. Great, he'd overstepped. "I'm sorry. I probably should apologize first for everything—"

She shook her head. "Don't apologize. I'd love to spend more time catching up, but I ... I'm seeing someone. I don't think that Kev would approve of my spending time with you ... alone." Her pale features pinked up as a blush filtered across her cheeks.

He shouldn't have been surprised. Ava was a beautiful woman. She was smart and she still had a sense of humor from what he had been able to gather. Ava was a catch. Max shook that thought aside as quickly as it had materialized. There had only been one moment in his life when he'd toyed with the thought of getting involved with Ava.

End of junior year. They'd been friends for so long, he had thought they might have a shot at being more. But then his life had turned upside down. It was probably for the best, because he would have never wanted to ruin their friendship in that way.

Max cleared his throat, hating how he hadn't recovered as quickly as he should have. "That's fine. How about I take the two of you out, my treat. I know this place you would probably love."

Ava stared at him for longer than he thought was necessary—long enough he nearly told her to forget it. But then she nodded, and her smile reappeared. "Sure. I'll check he's free but I bet Kev would go for that. When are you thinking?"

"I'm free tonight." Inwardly, he grimaced. That was not the way to show her that he wasn't crazy. "It's just that I have this charity thing I'm planning, and I'll be busy with that. We really start to push preparations next week. But if you're not available—"

"I think we can make it work." Her smile was like a ray of sunshine in an otherwise dismal day.

Max shoved his bleak thoughts aside and matched her

smile with one of his own. "Wonderful. I'll make the reservations and send you the information, if I may have your number?"

She wrote a number onto the side of his coffee cup with a grin.

"It was nice seeing you again, Max."

She slipped out of his office and he watched through the glass as she headed for the elevator. Ava waved at Cathy, who only responded with a short nod. And then she was gone.

For a moment he didn't move. This had to be one of the strangest mornings he'd had in a long time. Ava Brooks had walked back into his life after all these years.

And now they were going to have dinner.

Not a date. Just dinner.

With her and ... *Kev*.

His mouth dipped into a frown. For some reason that name just rubbed him the wrong way. Max spun around and headed for his desk. There was still a lot to do and Ava's arrival had knocked him off schedule. Time to get his head back in the game.

He settled in his desk chair, but as hard as he tried, he couldn't get his focus where it needed to be. His thoughts continued to drift to Ava. She was working at a coffee shop. She was dating a guy. What had happened to her dream of becoming a pastry chef?

She'd loved baking sweets and sharing them with anyone who was willing to become her guinea pig. Her cupcakes were the best he'd ever had, and he'd been all over the world.

The computer screen before him dimmed from inactivity and he pushed away from his desk to stare out the window again. As far as he could gather, she hadn't changed much. So why would she settle for a job in a coffee shop?

He was probably making too much out of this. Max needed to remember that there were reasons why people chose different paths and this one was none of his business. He'd had his own dreams until the money came into his mother's life and as a dependent, he'd had little choice but to adapt. Now though, he was happy. At least, he was happy to be in a position to help others and for the most part enjoyed his work.

Max pushed aside these thoughts. He really shouldn't be concerned about Ava. Sure, they'd been friends once upon a time, but that was it. She was dating someone for heaven's sake! He needed to show a respectful distance.

Yes, that's what he would do. He'd attend this dinner and that would be the end of it. "Cathy!" he called.

Within seconds she was at his door. "Yes, sir?"

"Please make a reservation at *Ruthie's* for this evening at six. Make sure they know I'm the one requesting the reservation, or they might not accept it."

She didn't move right away, her eyes drilling into him with what could only be described as curiosity and disappointment. "For two?"

"Three." He turned back to his computer. "Thank you," he dismissed her. Max didn't even bother looking up to see if she was gone. It was time to put Ava out of his mind and focus on what was more important.

❄

Max swirled the glass of ice water in his hand as he waited for Ava to arrive.

Ava and *Kev*.

His nose wrinkled simply thinking of the guy. The worst part was that this guy was probably really nice. Ava wouldn't give him the time of day otherwise. She would have found the best kind of person to date, and Max wouldn't be able to say a single bad thing about him.

The hum of voices and light instrumental music filled the

restaurant. Waitresses moved swiftly through the room, dodging tables and patrons who wandered to and from the tables.

The scent of spices and herbs inundated his senses, making his stomach growl. This place was popular mostly for the way they cooked their steaks, but Max came here for the garlic potatoes. Mouth watering, Max glanced once more at his watch. She'd be arriving soon.

He had only a few minutes to settle his racing heart. Being on edge wouldn't do him or her any favors. Max stared into his water, his brows drawn together and his jaw tight. For the remainder of the afternoon, he'd focused far too much on whether or not his mother had done something to prevent Ava's messages reaching him when he'd moved. It didn't really add up. And every time he wanted to blame his mother, a little voice reminded him that he hadn't exactly picked up a phone to call Ava.

"Max? I'm so sorry we're late. We couldn't find any parking."

Max lifted his gaze to find Ava, her cheeks flushed and breathing heavily. He glanced at his watch and chuckled. "You're not late. It's a minute after the hour." He got to his feet, a young man standing behind Ava catching his attention.

"*Technically*, we're a minute late." She pulled out her own chair and took her seat.

Kev eyed Max with distrust. His gaze locked onto Max's and he didn't take his seat right away.

Offering a smile, Max held out his hand. "Ava said great things about you."

"Yeah? That's funny. She hasn't said anything about you."

Max's focus bounced to Ava as she gave her boyfriend an exasperated look. "Kev! I told you about Max on the way here."

Kev didn't even glance in her direction. "Yeah, well, if he

was such a great friend, you would have talked about him before today."

Her face flushed a bright red color and she covered it with both of her hands. "I'm sure I mentioned him before."

"I don't think so." Kev crossed his arms, clearly not thrilled about having to be here.

Max became acutely aware he was still holding out his hand and quickly dropped it to his side. "Well, it's nice to meet you. Ava and I were friends in high school, but we haven't been in contact for years. Thanks for letting us catch up."

Ava snorted, muttering two words under her breath. "*Letting*? Hardly."

Max bit back a smile. Ava still had spunk. She was still just as quick-witted, and she was making it clear she wouldn't get pushed around. Her eyes cut to meet his and she grimaced as she settled into her seat. She didn't have to utter an apology. Somehow, he knew that was something she thought she needed to do, but she wasn't about to make her boyfriend feel like he wasn't respected. Instead, she picked up her menu and opened it to block her face.

Max gestured toward the seat beside Ava then sat in his own chair. "I don't usually have a good reason to come here."

Ava peered at him over the edge of her menu. "The food looks delicious."

"It is. Shall we order?"

❈

Over dinner the conversation was pleasant enough and the meal was melt-in-your-mouth good. The minutes the plates were cleared, Kev cleared his throat a bit loudly.

"So, Mr. Stone, why don't you fill me in on your history with Ava? All I have to go off are the stories from reporters and the vague stuff Ava spit out on the way here."

Max cocked his head slightly, taking in this man who practically dripped with disdain. He sat a little too close to Ava and it was more than obvious there was a thread of jealousy tied around him. Ironically, the man had nothing to be jealous about. Max was far too busy for a relationship, even if the thought had tempted him earlier today. "There isn't much to tell. I grew up going to the same school as Ava. You could say we both lived on the wrong side of the tracks."

Kev snorted derisively. "You expect me to believe you grew up in what was basically the projects of Georgia?"

"I wouldn't lie about something like that."

"Many men before you have lied about that very thing to get the approval of the average man."

"*Kevin!*" Ava hissed. She shook her head but didn't say anything further.

"What? The guy is a gazillionaire. People like him don't just magically get money. It takes generations to build what he has."

"It did." Max gave Kev a wry smile. "Unfortunately, the family that worked to build this wealth wasn't involved with raising me. Sorry to disappoint you, but I did grow up very poor."

Ava's cheeks were still flushed to the point she looked like she'd been outside in the sun without any protection for several hours.

Kev stared at Max, the disbelief easily read on his face.

At any other meeting, Max might have chuckled to ease the tension in the air. But this man seated across from him had stolen any desire to be cordial at all. He'd been willing to give the man the benefit of the doubt, but not anymore. Even a guy who was jealous could maintain a polite front, if only to remain on his girlfriend's good side.

Ava had managed to find someone who was so far beneath her that she could step over him.

"Enough about me. How about you? What do you do for work, Kev?"

"I'm a contractor. Real men's work. None of this hiding behind a desk and doling out money whenever I see fit. I have to solve problems the old-fashioned way."

Ava shot out of her seat and glowered at him. "For heaven's sake, Kev—"

"It's fine, Ava," Max murmured, though secretly the glee that filled him over this little encounter was taking over his whole body.

"No, it's not okay," she shot at him without looking. "Kev, can I have a word with you?"

Kev didn't move.

"Alone?"

Max got up from his seat. "You know what? I need to use the restroom anyway." He strode away from the table without waiting for Ava to respond. He wasn't interested in sticking around for this conversation any more than he would have wanted the press to show up unannounced.

And as much as he wanted Ava to put the guy in his place, he also didn't want to see her hurting just because their paths had crossed again after all these years.

Chapter Four

Ava whirled on the man she'd thought she knew. Kev had his flaws for sure, but he'd never shown his jealousy to this degree before. "What was that?"

He slumped deeper into his seat. "What was what?"

She threw down her menu and glowered at him. "You know exactly what I'm talking about. You never treat people like that."

"I've never had to meet someone who was clearly trying to steal you away from me."

Ava gasped. "Max is *not* trying to do anything. He was my *best friend* when we were younger. We drifted apart. Now we're reconnecting. What is so hard to understand about that?"

Kev gave her one of those looks that always made her feel like an idiot. That was one thing he was very good at. With a single look he could make her feel like she'd done something wrong or said something stupid. That was the biggest thing she disliked about him.

But she'd been raised to believe that no one was perfect and just because he had that *one* fault didn't mean she should

THE COOKIE MATCH

just break up with him. Now, it looked like there were two things she didn't approve of. If he couldn't get this jealous streak taken care of, then perhaps it was time they discussed no longer being in a relationship.

This wasn't the first time she'd thought about breaking up with him, and it made her feel sick to her stomach. Not because she couldn't handle being on her own. She could definitely take care of herself. She'd done so for several years. But because it suddenly was clear that if she'd thought about exiting the relationship more than once, she needed to do it.

Ava dragged her fingers down her face, hating how flushed she felt. "Everything you said was highly inappropriate. You're acting like a crazy person."

"Am I? Because the way I see it, that guy only invited you here tonight so he could hit on you. I seemed more like an afterthought."

"I *told* you. He invited both of us."

Kev let out a sharp bark of laughter. "You can't possibly expect me to believe that. I'm not blind, Ava. I saw the way he looked at you the second you arrived. I've seen the way he is on TV and I have never seen him more happy than when you showed up."

His statement gave her pause. She hadn't noticed any of that. But then again, they'd been late, and she always hated when she wasn't punctual. Rather than dwell on what Kev said, she lowered herself back into her chair and fixed him with a warning look. "You need to behave yourself."

"Or what? Honestly, I'd rather not be here at all. I'd be thrilled if you said we were leaving and we wouldn't have to see him ever again."

Her eyes narrowed. "Do you seriously think that this is the last time I'm going to visit with him?"

That question shocked him. She saw the exact moment the realization hit him and for a moment she thought she could see his skin turn a sickly shade of green, before flushing red like hers must have been. "I'm not going to let you see him again. If that's your plan, then you might as well break up with me right now."

Her eyes widened, but she didn't give him any other indication that his words were a shock to her senses. She'd had some past relationships that had ended badly, but never before had any man she'd dated attempted to control her the way Kev was doing right now.

Each and every bad dating experience came rushing to the surface, flooding her memories with their bitter taste. Try as she might, she couldn't get them to stop swirling angrily in her head. "Then leave," she whispered.

"What?"

"You heard me," she said more firmly this time. "You can go. I'm not going to date someone who won't at least show me enough respect to trust me. I've brushed aside several little things about you that are probably red flags and I think it's just about time that I cut you loose anyway."

Kev lowered his voice, presumably so the surrounding tables didn't hear him. His face was now almost a shade of purple. "You're breaking up with me because of him, aren't you?"

Ava shook her head. "No, I'm breaking up with you because of me. I'm worth *more*."

Kev snorted. "You must think I'm an idiot."

She was beginning to realize just that.

"But I'm not, you know. I get what's going on. You're moving on to greener pastures because the great Maximus Stone has eyes for you. Well guess what? It won't last, sweetheart. The guy is notorious for keeping the women in his life at arm's length. I've read all the articles you have. He's a playboy. He won't even give his mother the time of day."

"Just because the tabloids—"

Kev shook his head. "My mate's wife works at Maple Gardens. She says he only ever visits like three times a year. Mother's Day, Christmas, and family day. And sometimes not even all of them. Heck, he doesn't even see her on her birthday. Is that the kind of guy you're interested in dating?"

Ava continued to scowl at Kev. She had heard the rumors, but she wasn't about to put stock in most of them. But if what Kev said was true, then he'd made a good point. Family was important to her. Nothing should cause the kind of rift Kev was talking about. He was just trying to put doubt into her head.

He shot up from his seat then shoved it hard against the table. "You'll see. His true colors will show eventually and you'll come crawling back."

"In your dreams," she muttered.

"What?"

"Goodbye, Kev."

His lips curled with disgust. "Don't be disappointed when you find out *I've* moved on to greener pastures." With that last statement, he marched away from the table.

She wasn't about to follow him. Her relationship with Kev hadn't been perfect. She knew that. But that didn't stop her from caring about him. A girl didn't spend months of her life dating a guy, expecting it to come to an end over an old friend. Was it love, though? Her heart ached. It had been sharp at first, then pulsed dully after that, much like when she'd hit her funny bone on the molding of a doorway. Now all she felt was an unpleasant tingling sensation.

If she did love him, it hadn't been the kind of love she'd wanted since she was a child. Where was the magic? Did it even exist?

The pain in her palms was the first thing that pulled her out of her thoughts. She glanced down to find four angry crescent marks in each hand. They were dark at first, then shifted to a bright red. Ava tilted her hands, opening and closing her fists until she heard the scratch of the wooden chair across from her dragging across the floor.

She glanced up to find Max settling into his chair. He picked up the menu and flipped it open as if it were the most natural thing in the world. And maybe it was. Max definitely noticed that Kev was missing. And yet he was acting as if nothing had changed.

"We should order. Ooh. The trifle looks good. Have you ever had it?"

She lifted a brow. "Seriously?"

Max glanced up at her over the small menu. "Right. You've never been here before. Well, I've had the crème brûlée, but I've always wanted to try the cookie ice cream."

"That's not what I meant and you know it."

He put the menu down and pointed at the item. "It's got chocolate and whipped cream. You used to love that stuff when we were younger."

"Max," she murmured. There was no avoiding the conversation. It wasn't like they could just pretend that Kev had disappeared. And she wasn't the kind of person to let Max walk on eggshells around her. "You can go ahead and ask. I'm not going to get upset."

"I might not have seen you for the better part of ten years, but I can tell you that I know you're lying."

"Max!"

He picked up a breadstick and pointed it at her. "I don't think I've ever seen you this upset in all the time I've known you."

She crossed her arms, leaning back in her seat as she muttered, "You didn't see me after you left." Ava had thought she'd been quiet enough, especially beneath the hum of conversation around them, but apparently not.

Max stilled, the breadstick halfway to his mouth. He

didn't look at her directly, while he obviously tried to come up with something he could say to her.

Well, that was just great. She'd managed to make Max uncomfortable. They'd been doing just fine until Kevin had to go and ruin everything and now she was stuck sitting across from a man who was little more than a stranger to her.

Ava let her gaze sweep through the room, hating how the guilt over her statement consumed her. It wasn't Max's fault that he left when he did. Deep down, she knew that better than anyone. Maybe Max hadn't gotten the memo. The way he went quiet made it perfectly clear that he wasn't over what had transpired between them either.

This was shaping up to be one of the top least-favorite moments in her life. It might even come close to the day when Max had abandoned their friendship for good.

Ava peeked at him, then jumped a little when she found his gaze on her. The way those eyes drilled into her made her flinch again.

"I didn't want to move, Ava."

"I know," she said it quietly, but this time she knew better than to assume he couldn't hear her.

"I would have stayed if I could have."

"I *know*," she repeated. "But it doesn't change the fact that it happened. You disappeared on me at one of the lowest points of my life. My mom died from cancer and I had to move in with my grandmother. That was when I first called you to tell you my new phone number. It was ... *hard*."

This time he looked away. What if he shared his suspicions that his mother had deliberately not passed on her messages? It wouldn't accomplish anything other than to make it look like he was passing the buck. "Well, it seems like you managed just fine without me."

Ava snorted.

His eyes flitted to hers. "You were always good at that, you know. I don't know anyone else who has such a knack for coming out on top when the chips are down. It's something I admired about you."

Warmth started as a small flicker in the pit of her stomach and swiftly moved to other parts of her body. She offered him a smile. "Don't you know? Flattery will get you everywhere."

Max put down the breadstick and tapped the menu that still was splayed open between them. "Does that mean you'll split the ice cream with me?"

She shook her head. "I'm not sharing a single morsel of it with the likes of you. I'm getting one all for myself."

Chapter Five

Max placed his spoon into the empty bowl. That was the best dessert he'd ever tried in his life, and he'd been all over the world.

Ava still pecked at hers, only half of it gone.

"So much for eating one all on your own," he laughed.

She stuck out her tongue, then took an oversized bite. Her eyes widened and she covered her mouth with her fingertips, eliciting another chuckle from him.

Max's focus shifted to the empty chair beside her. It was pretty obvious Kev wasn't coming back. Max was too realistic to believe that they'd broken up over such an insignificant argument. But he didn't know Kev and the man might have been on thin ice to begin with.

Still, Max burned with several questions. Had Kev opted to go home and cool off? Or were they really severing ties? He couldn't exactly ask Ava about any of it. Who were they to each other after all these years? Definitely not friends—not in the way they once were.

And yet, he couldn't seem to help himself.

"I feel like Kev leaving is my fault."

Her eyes darted up to meet his. "Why on earth would that be your fault?"

He shrugged as he shifted in his seat and clasped his hands on the table in front of him. "Because he was upset I was here. And then he left."

Ava rolled her eyes. "It's not your fault what other people do. You can't control anyone."

"But you could've gone with him." He probably shouldn't have pointed that out, but again, he was making a lot of decisions he probably needed to reevaluate when it came to this conversation.

"Yes, I could have. But I didn't."

"And why is that?" There was a brief shimmer of a moment when he thought she might say that it had to do with him. In a fairy tale, that's exactly what she'd do. Ava would confess their friendship had always been more to her, just like he'd wanted it to be when they were younger. Then she'd tell him that meeting up was the sign she needed to get out of the awful relationship with Kev. Despite the ridiculousness of that train of thought, it showed Max one thing.

He still had feelings for her.

Ava blew out a heavy breath as she glanced toward him. "Because I've realized something."

Max's heart sped up in a way he hadn't experienced for years. This wasn't happening. Ava was too levelheaded to jump from one relationship to the other, no matter how much Max might want it. He fidgeted in his seat, scooting a little closer to her.

"Dating isn't worth it."

That ... was unexpected.

"I'm swearing off relationships for the undetermined future. I'm tired of investing my time in something that isn't going to turn out the way I hope. The way I *need*." She ran a hand through her hair and sighed again. "See? My life isn't perfect."

"I ... never said it was."

Her eyes shot to meet his and she let out a strained laugh. "Right."

Max continued to watch her, half hoping that she'd take back what she'd said and tell him it was all a joke. This wasn't the girl he remembered. The Ava he knew would roll with the punches and dive back into life without a second thought. But the woman in front of him didn't do any of that. While she didn't appear depressed, nor was she lingering on what she'd just gone through, she was clearly hurt. He wanted to climb into the seat beside her and give her a hug, but somehow that didn't seem like the right thing to do.

Ava met his gaze and an embarrassed smile reappeared on her lips. "I'm sorry. I can't believe you got to have a front-row seat to my personal life." She covered her face with her hands then splayed her fingers so she could look at him through them. "Next topic, okay? Can we just ... talk about something else?"

And there she was again. The bright, happy woman he remembered. She'd pushed past this brief moment of insecurity. He couldn't figure out if it was for her sake or for his that she'd made the effort. Perhaps it was both.

Max nodded. "Okay. Something else." He searched the room as if it would give him some idea of what they could discuss. Her dating life was off the table. Kev was most definitely a no. His gaze landed on the dessert in front of her and he gestured toward it. "You still perfecting your culinary skills?"

She glanced at the dessert and her features froze. She didn't frown, but her smile seemed like it had been painted on her face. "I can't believe you remember that."

"Of course I remember it. You made delicious desserts."

She snorted. "I made you cookies and cupcakes."

"No, I remember that one time you tried your hand at eclairs."

Her eyes brightened, even though her smile didn't. "And that was a disaster."

"No, it wasn't. They were the best eclairs I'd had up until that point."

Ava laughed this time. "Of course. But now you've been all over the world. Why wouldn't you try the real thing?"

"The real thing?"

"Yeah, haven't you been to Paris? I bet you had them there, right?"

Max shook his head. "Do you think I have time to wander the streets looking for authentic food?"

She shrugged. "Based on what *I* remember, food was the only thing that spoke to you."

Quiet fell between them as a crooked smile crossed his face. It wasn't any wonder why he'd loved spending time with her—why he'd wanted to catch up. Every memory came rushing back. The late nights they spent in her kitchen making snacks after a long day were some of his favorite times.

"Yeah, I suppose you're right." He pushed the bowl away. "How about you make me one of your signature treats."

Her expression faltered. "I haven't baked in ... well, in a long time."

"You haven't?"

She shook her head.

"Why not?"

"You should know that better than anyone. Work. Relationships. That stuff takes energy."

He leaned forward, his gaze searching hers. "That sure sounds like an excuse."

Ava could have been offended at his statement. Heck, he probably would have been upset if someone accused him of avoiding something he'd once dreamed of doing. Baking had been that dream to Ava once upon a time, but something had changed. Was it losing her mom?

Thankfully, she didn't appear at all upset. Instead, she chuckled. "You can think what you want. I like my job. I'm living a comfortable life. I don't need to go chasing a childish dream."

"Well, why the heck not?"

She sobered. "What?"

"Why aren't you chasing after a dream you would have excelled at?"

"Now you're sounding just like my grandmother."

Max straightened. "Sounds like your grandmother and I would get along."

"You probably would," she shot back. "But the fact of the matter is that I don't have any interest in baking anymore."

"Really?" His voice was flat and devoid of belief.

"Really," she said. "Besides, even if I was interested, I'm out of practice." Ava picked at the fibers on the tablecloth and looked away. "Man, you have a habit of bringing up difficult subjects."

"What's so difficult about asking what you want to do when you grow up?"

She snickered. "I'm an adult, Max. I don't have any more growing up to do. How about we turn the spotlight on you? How does your mother feel about your relationship status? Hmm? I'm guessing she had expected to have grandbabies by now."

Her words stung more than he cared to admit. She was right. Lily had never hidden that she was looking forward to the day when he'd find someone to love. Even after she'd moved into Maple Gardens, she'd brought it up occasionally.

Lucky for him, she didn't have a say in that sort of thing—at least not anymore. He'd find a woman on his terms in his own time. Max let out a soft laugh and waved a dismissive hand through the air. "Touché. No more personal questions."

Once again, their conversation dwindled. He couldn't help but feel like this get-together had run its course. Ava didn't seem to want to spend any more time with him than was necessary, but he hadn't given her an excuse to leave.

Max should just accept that this friendship wasn't what it once was. Just because they bumped into each other didn't mean that they could pick up where they'd left off. He raked his hand across his face and released a pent-up breath. "I suppose I should let you get going. I'm sure you have plenty of better things to do."

She cocked her head, her eyes dancing with a familiar mischief. "Are you trying to get out of our dinner date?"

Date? This wasn't a date.

Was it?

No. Of course not. She'd come with her boyfriend for heaven's sake. Not only that, but she'd just said she was swearing off relationships.

The look on his face must have been something else, because she threw back her head and laughed. "You need to lighten up, Max. And there's no need to cut tonight short. I could use the distraction."

"You ... want to ... continue spending time with me?"

She shrugged. "I can't think of a better way to spend the rest of my evening after breaking up with my boyfriend than to spend it with an old friend."

There used to be a time when her sentiment would have thrilled him. He used to search for any excuse possible to spend even another five minutes with Ava. And she wanted to do just that. The best part was that he hadn't requested it. "One condition."

Her brows furrowed and a flash of uncertainty crossed her features. "What's that?"

"I'd love for you to make me something sweet to eat."

"Aren't you full? I'm sure you said you were."

"I won't be in half an hour. I'm still like I was as a teen. Ready to eat at the drop of a hat."

Ava rolled her eyes. "I told you—"

"It's like riding a bike, right? You should be able to pick up a spatula and—"

"A *spatula*?" She laughed. "I don't remember ever using a spatula when I made stuff before."

Max searched his mind for the right term. He could have sworn that was the right word. "You know, one of those silicone, rubbery things that help you scrape a bowl clean?"

"I know what a spatula *is*, Max. But I never used one when we were kids." She laughed again. "How do you even know what it is? With your kind of money, I would have thought you'd have hired help to do the stuff in the kitchen. Speaking of which, you can't tell me that you don't have a personal chef or someone who can already make you a dessert any time you snap your fingers."

"Actually, I don't."

She snapped her mouth shut and her eyes widened slightly. "*What?*"

"I don't have a personal chef." He said it simply enough. Yes, once upon a time he had hired someone to prepare his meals for him, but he'd long since been the only one responsible for his food. There were just too many important things he needed to use his money for—usually to prepare for the next charity event. Those weren't cheap and while they raised money, he still had to front the cost for the staff who helped him with each one.

"You're kidding." Her voice broke through his reverie.

"What reason would I have for lying about something like that?"

She shrugged. "I dunno."

"Well, I'm not. The only person I have working for me back home is a housekeeper and that's mostly so I don't have to bother with the vacuuming. I still hate that." He bit back a laugh. "Anyway, what do you say? For old time's sake?"

Ava stared at him. He must not have been very convincing because she didn't appear the least bit interested in cooking for him. Who could blame her? She'd just broken up with a guy she'd probably been in love with.

"Fine."

He stilled, her answer throwing him off guard. "Fine?"

She stood, gathered her purse and jerked her head toward the door. "But we have to get a few things first."

Chapter Six

Ava watched, bemused, as Max placed one foot on the shopping cart bar in front of him and pushed it along the aisle with his other foot. "You're going to tip that over, you know that, right?"

"And if I do, you can kiss me better." He said it flippantly but, nevertheless, it seemed to hit a chord inside her. Once upon a time she'd had such a crush on him and boy did it run *deep*. So many times she'd nearly confessed the whole thing, but that would have destroyed the relationship they'd had.

Well, the joke was on her. Their relationship—the friendship that it was—had been ruined anyway. Ava had to pick up her pace a little in order to keep up with him as they darted along the mostly vacant aisles of the nearest grocery store. There were just a few things she had to get if she was going to make him a dessert that would have him begging for more. He deserved to be tortured, after the dinner he'd put her through.

A wry smile crossed her lips as she admonished herself. He wasn't the problem. That had all been Kev. But if he hadn't asked her to dinner, then perhaps none of this would have happened anyway.

"What are we looking for?" Max called over his shoulder, already half an aisle ahead of her again.

"I need lemons. And some eggs."

"What are you making?" Max stopped, turned his cart around and pushed off again toward her. But this time he didn't account for the speed with which he started, and the front wheels of the cart lifted off the ground.

The wire frame rose higher and higher as if in slow motion. Max's expression went from surprise to shock to bordering on terror, which only caused a burst of laughter to bubble from Ava's chest.

She doubled over, her hands on her knees trying to remain in control of her bodily functions as Max landed with a clatter on the ground.

Only one onlooker noticed, and his reaction was just as priceless. He had to be nearing his eighties and, boy, was he unimpressed. His white bushy eyebrows lowered with disdain and he shook his head as he moved past them.

Ava laughed again, rushing over to where Max lay, her laughter getting even louder. "I told you that you were going to fall."

Max sat up, pushing the cart off him as he glanced around. His own expression was one of disbelief, but mostly just bitterness. His grumpy demeanor had returned.

She held out her hand toward him, still unable to contain the chuckles that escaped her lips. "Are you okay?"

"No," he muttered.

"You sound like a toddler."

His eyes darted up toward her, but they were hard. "You'd be upset, too, if the cart tipped over on you."

"No," she drawled, "I wouldn't be riding it like a skateboard to begin with." She wiggled her fingers to bring attention to the fact she'd offered to help him up.

Max glanced at her hand, then back to her face. If she

didn't know any better, she might think he was ready to push out his lower lip and pout at her.

She snickered, dropping both hands to her knees. "Do you need me to kiss you better?" She referenced his earlier statement and that seemed to get his attention.

One side of his mouth quirked upward and he lifted his elbow. "Right there."

Ava rolled her eyes, though the amusement was still there. She crouched down beside him and pressed a kiss to his elbow.

He pointed to his shoulder. "There."

Again, she obliged.

Next Max pointed to his cheek. Ava hesitated, then sighed. It was just his cheek. She grazed it so lightly she doubted he could even feel it from beneath the scruff that grew there. But when he pointed to his lower lip she gave him a flat look. "No."

"But I hurt it."

With that, she shoved his forehead with the palm of her hand, nearly knocking him off balance. "Nice try, buddy. But when I said I was swearing off guys, I meant it." She got to her feet and straightened her shirt out of habit. Then she righted the cart and nodded toward a nearby shelf. "The vanilla extract is up there. Let's get this stuff and get out of here before we get kicked out for public indecency."

Ava pushed past him, biting back a smile as he hurried after her.

"It's not public indecency, you know. It'd be a public display of affection and as long as it's not lewd it would have been just fine."

"You're still at it, huh?" Ava chuckled. "Well, maybe I need to find you someone who would be willing to kiss a toad if it meant being with the prince later down the line. But that just isn't me."

His eyes widened then he grinned. "Was that just a compliment you paid me?"

"Nope." Ava was lying through her teeth and she knew it. Max was a good guy. He was charming and handsome, among other things. Any girl would be lucky to be the one he fell for. They'd just have to get past his brooding nature—something she didn't have the time or patience to do.

Max jumped in front of her, his hands wrapping around the edge of the shopping cart to prevent her from running from this conversation. "Admit it. You think I'm a prince."

She rolled her eyes. "I think you're full of it."

"Okay, you think I'm handsome."

"Anyone with eyes could see that." She said it before she had a chance to analyze what it might sound like to Max. By the time she did, it was too late.

Max grinned ear to ear. "You think I'm handsome."

She let out a groan, pushing the cart harder. "If this was what I was missing out on when you left, then maybe it was for the best." Ava got past him, laughing at his disgruntled response.

"*Hey!*" His laughter joined hers as they continued on through the store and to the checkout counter.

Max paid for their supplies and they headed toward his car. He opened the trunk and grabbed the bags, but she must have had a funny kind of look on her face because he stopped. A nervous smile crossed his face as he brought the back of the trunk down with a resounding *thunk*. "What?"

She straightened, shaking her head as she schooled her features. "Nothing."

"That's not nothing. Why do I get the feeling that you're judging me?"

Ava laughed. "Because maybe I am. Though, it's not as bad as you might think." She moved around to the side of the

THE COOKIE MATCH

car to climb in but he placed his hand on the door to stop her. "What did I do this time?"

She gestured toward the car. "Okay, so it just occurred to me that you're driving yourself around. A bit slow, I know, seeing as you drove me here."

"I do have a license to drive," he said.

Another laugh spilled from her chest. She hadn't laughed this much in a long time. In fact, the last time she felt this carefree had been when they were kids. It was ... nice. "What I mean is that I would have expected you to have a driver and a limo."

Something flickered across his features, but it was too quick for her to get a read on it. It wasn't a *happy* something, either. She might have very well offended him by her statement.

"I'm not going to waste money on having someone drive me around town. Heck, when we were kids we took the bus everywhere, or don't you remember?"

"Oh, I'm very aware." She lifted a shoulder in an attempt to shrug off the embarrassment she felt over making such an assumption. "I just figured with your money ..."

"My *money*? The money I have I use to help others." His tone was light, but she couldn't help feeling he was being somewhat defensive.

"Okay, sheesh. But what about your car?" Her eyes drifted to the vehicle that likely cost more than he would ever admit to. She'd been inside. It had all the bells and whistles.

He stared at her, unmoving. Then his shoulders dropped and he raked a hand through his hair. The sheepish grin on his face made the last several moments worth it. "Touché."

"Darn straight, touché. That's what I'm talking about."

"So I'm not gonna get *any* credit?"

"I mean ... there was probably a limo driver who could have used a job."

He let out a low whistle. "You know right where to hit, don't you?" Max shook his head as he grasped the handle and pulled the door open for her. "Remind me never to get into a debate with you."

If she wasn't so caught off guard by him acting the gentleman, she might have thrown another snarky comment at him. But in this moment all she could think about was that Kev hadn't opened her door since their first date.

This isn't a date.

They were not going to continue spending time together after tonight, because he had a life and she didn't fit into it. There was no need for her to get attached or to fall into the trap of wanting to hang with him.

They weren't *friends*. Not anymore. They were *friendly*.

Just because he wanted to come back to her place didn't mean a single thing.

She took her seat and peered up at him as he rested his elbow on the door and gave her a small smile. It was a ghost of the ones he used to wear before he moved away. None of his smiles this evening had been like the ones she remembered. Perhaps she was being too hard on him. He'd gone through his own stuff, too.

"Thank you," she murmured.

"For what?"

She shrugged. "For being my friend, I guess."

He nodded stiffly. "It's easy being your friend, Ava. Always has been." With that he shut the door and walked around to his side of the car.

The ride to her place was quiet. The music was low enough for them to have a conversation, but she wasn't up for talking. The air between them had been tainted somehow. It was like she didn't know how to be his friend anymore. Anything she might say to him could be taken the wrong way.

THE COOKIE MATCH

Ava peeked at him out of the corner of her eye, then let out a sigh. Max walking back into her life after so long was definitely nothing like she would have expected.

Chapter Seven

Max followed Ava up to the front door, somewhat surprised at the home where she now resided. The neighborhood where they'd grown up had left its mark on him and he'd never wanted to go back.

Except to see Ava again. The more time he spent with her, the more he wondered why on earth he hadn't made more of an effort —any effort, into visiting her.

This place, it was like the homes they'd dreamed of moving into as kids. It wasn't run down; the neighborhood was nice. Ava had moved up in the world—but that could have been all due to her grandmother taking her in.

Ava didn't chat with him. Her normal bubbly conversation had died with the end of their talk of money. Why did the subject have to create such a divide between them? It didn't seem fair. It had already stolen their past, now it was going to steal their future?

What future?

A voice in his head mocked him. They didn't have a future. He was too busy for relationships and Ava had already said she was swearing off relationships. His only shot at keeping her as a small part of his future would be to ensure they remained friends, no matter what differences separated them.

She pulled out her keys and shoved one into the lock. Funny how something so mundane was something he didn't deal with. Yes, he chose not to be extravagant with his money, but he did have some things that he considered necessities.

The lock on his door was electronic. There was no worry of losing his keys or having someone break in that way. He had a state-of-the-art security system, but that came with the house.

She pushed herself into the darkened house. Her hand flew out to the side and she flipped on a switch that illuminated a foyer with a sitting room that didn't look like it'd been used in a decade. Ava glanced at him over her shoulder, then jerked her head toward the hallway. "The kitchen's this way."

He shut the door behind him, drinking in the place where Ava had spent the last several years of her life. She hadn't mentioned her mother or her grandmother other than mentioning what had happened when he left, and he didn't want to push it.

Ava's home was tidy, and well-kept, but there was something about it that didn't feel quite right. It was as if he were walking into someone else's home and Ava just lived there.

"Ava? Is that you?"

Max jumped in place then spun around to stare at an older woman as she headed down the stairs. There was a familiarity about her—something he couldn't place—until Ava backtracked into the hallway.

The two women could have been sisters, if there wasn't such a big age gap. Max had met Ava's mother and this wasn't her. That meant the woman standing at the foot of the stairs had to be Ava's grandmother.

He watched with keen interest as Ava hurried to the

woman's side and gave her a hug. "Hey, Nana. I'm just going to bake something in the kitchen. We promise not to be too loud."

Ava's nana shot a curious look in Max's direction. "I thought you went out with Kev."

Ava sighed. "Long story. This is Max. The guy I was telling you about earlier."

Understanding flooded her features. "Your friend from high school."

"Yep."

She leaned into Ava and whispered, though it was still loud enough for Max to hear every word. "He's cuter than Kev."

"Nana!" Ava laughed. "We're just friends. I don't think I'm going to be dating for a while—a *long* while."

Her grandmother shot her a concerned look but didn't press the issue probably due to Max's presence. Instead, she smiled broadly and moved toward him, her hand outstretched. "I'm Rosalie and I expect you to use my name. I've heard so much about you, but I didn't realize you were *the* Maximus Stone that I see in the news. You are even more handsome than your pictures."

"*Nana*," Ava repeated with exasperation.

"What? He is. I wish you would have told me he was the one you were talking about."

Ava dragged a hand down her face. "Like I said, we're just going to make some cookies then he's going home. We're just catching up, that's all."

"Catching up, after you broke up with your boyfriend?"

A groan burst from Ava's lips. She shook her head, then sent an apologetic look to Max. Mouthing the word *sorry*, she attempted to turn her grandmother back toward the stairs, but she wouldn't budge.

"If she's making you cookies then you must have tried her desserts before."

Max nodded, unable to hide his amusement that this woman was so intent on sticking around. "Once upon a time I told her she should open up her own bakery."

Rosalie elbowed Ava in the ribs, eliciting a yelp and a dark look. "See? That's what I've been saying all these years. You need to get yourself out of that coffee shop and make something of yourself."

Ava glanced at Max all too briefly. "We've been over this. I like my job. My boss is nice and I get to make sweets there."

"I'd hardly call croissants and muffins sweets. They're pastries, sure, but they're nothing compared to the stuff you make at home." Rosalie turned to Max, her expression bright. "Did you ever try her macarons? They're simply to die for. I don't think I've ever tasted something that can melt in your mouth and yet have a crisp texture at the same time."

Max glanced in Ava's direction, not surprised to find her avoiding his gaze. She hadn't been the type to draw attention to herself when they were younger and apparently that hadn't changed much over the years. "I haven't."

"Well, it's your lucky day, you get to have some tonight," she muttered. "Nana, it's getting late. You really ought to be in bed. I'll make sure to clean up everything and leave you a few cookies, too, okay?"

Rosalie winked at Max. "I can see when I'm not wanted. It was a pleasure to meet you, Max." She turned and took three steps before she stopped and faced them again.

Ava looked like she was about to burst from embarrassment.

"Max, dear, may I ask you something?"

"Sure."

Ava pinched the bridge of her nose and groaned again,

muttering something about regretting all of her decisions today.

"I read somewhere that you're hosting another charity something or other locally coming up soon."

"That's correct. It's an auction to help raise money for adoption agencies, foster families, and a connection program I've developed to link children who were removed from their homes with their parents."

"Lovely." She dropped down a step, her hand holding tight to the railing. "I seem to recall an article stating you have hired a local chef from a retirement community to cater the event, is that also correct?"

Max chuckled. "You seem to know a lot more than you've been letting on."

"Oh, I make it my business to know these sorts of things." Her smile lines deepened as she moved yet another step closer to him. "I was wondering if you've got all the help you need for your event—catering wise."

Ava must have caught on to what her grandmother was going to say before Max, because she jumped forward, blocking Max from her grandmother's approach. "No. Absolutely not. I told you that I'm not interested."

Max's eyes darted from Ava, up to Rosalie. "She's not interested in what?"

Nana waved her hand dismissively. "She's just scared. Both of us know that she's talented in the kitchen, right?"

"Of course."

"Max, come on, let's go make those cookies."

Rosalie continued as if Ava hadn't said a thing. "And if she were to be given a chance to showcase her abilities, it wouldn't be difficult at all to make a name for herself."

"Sure." Max bit back a smile as he watched color flood Ava's cheeks.

"Nana. This isn't the right time." Ava turned to plead

THE COOKIE MATCH

with her grandmother, but the older woman darted to the side.

"If that chef of yours specializes in the more savory dishes, wouldn't it be smart to hire someone else who can cover the desserts?"

That's when it dawned on him what this was about. Ava wasn't going to ask to help or to get hired. Her decision not to more than likely had something to do with her ego. But her grandmother had no problem with bringing up the topic.

Max stared at Ava with fresh eyes. Her nana was right, of course. Peter had a lot on his plate with preparing the menu, hiring staff, and getting the food prepped for this event. It was one of the biggest ones Max had planned thus far.

And Ava would be an excellent addition to the team. She could head the pastries and desserts blindfolded and with one hand behind her back. He beamed at her, but before he could utter a word she held up both hands.

"Before you say anything, like I told Nana, I'm not interested."

"How do you know you're not interested until you try it?"

Her hands dropped and her face scrunched with frustration. "That's what you say when you're trying new foods. This is different."

Max shook his head, shoving his hands into his pockets as he kept his gaze trained on her. "On the contrary, people say that exact same thing with *experiences*, too. Don't you think this kind of experience would fall under the same umbrella? You've never done something like this before—unless I'm missing something." He briefly met Rosalie's smug gaze and she shook her head. "There you go, then. This would be a wonderful opportunity for you."

"It's not about the *opportunity*." Ava threw her hands into the air and sighed. "Why are you guys ganging up on me?"

Rosalie placed a hand on her shoulder and murmured

softly, "Because we know you would be great." Her words were enough that even Max got goose bumps.

He shrugged as he rocked back on his heels. "Obviously we wouldn't force you to do something you really don't want to do. Perhaps you could take a day to think about it. There would be zero risk."

"Yeah, that's what you think," she muttered.

"What was that, dear?" Rosalie inched closer.

Ava's smile didn't reach her eyes as she looked up at her grandmother. "I guess I'll think about it."

"Wonderful. Now, you two don't stay up too late. I'm going to bed." She gave Max a little wave then took her leave.

Max was still watching her when Ava grabbed his elbow and yanked him down the hallway and into the kitchen. The only light was from the clock on the oven. She all but pushed him against the wall and wagged a finger in his face. "Why did you have to go and do that?"

He held up both hands, chuckling as he did so. "Do what? I didn't *do* anything."

"Yes, you did. You enabled her."

"What?" This time he laughed. "You're not making any sense."

"Nana has been trying for ages to get me to quit working at the coffee shop and try starting a bakery out of our kitchen."

"And why haven't you?"

Her mouth shut so quickly he wouldn't have been surprised if she'd bitten her tongue in the process.

Max tilted his head slightly, studying her. "Why haven't you started a bakery, Ava?" he asked again.

She shrugged, stepping back from him.

"That's not an answer."

"I know," she said. "I don't have an answer." She grabbed the bag of groceries she must have tossed into the kitchen

THE COOKIE MATCH

when they'd arrived, before her grandmother interrupted them.

One by one, she placed the items on the counter then she hurried across the room to flip on the lights.

The room illuminated so quickly it made Max wince. When his eyes found their focus, he watched Ava continue to gather the ingredients for their cookies. She didn't speak, nor did she find his gaze. This topic of conversation was one she apparently wasn't ready to have and he wasn't close enough to force her to.

Max shrugged out of his suit coat and draped it over a kitchen chair. Then he took out his cufflinks and rolled up his dress shirt sleeves.

Ava glanced at him for just a moment when he came up beside her at the stove. "What can I do to help?"

Chapter Eight

Ava's heart fluttered wildly in her chest. If she'd been pressed, she would have said she had zero feelings for Max. Even when they were teenagers, a relationship just never seemed like the right fit.

They were good together—just not in any way that people said they ought to be.

The ironic thing was that even after all these years, she had a sinking suspicion that Max still knew her better than even Kev had. Max knew her dreams and desires. He knew when she was lying. So, did he know when she was afraid? But he was wrong. Ava wasn't afraid. She refused to believe that.

Her disinterest in starting a bakery was nothing more than that—a disinterest. She didn't know what she wanted to do with her life. Was that so bad? Why couldn't she just stay in her job, content to be mediocre? Not everyone needed to excel at everything.

"Ava," Max whispered.

She jumped, hating how she'd allowed herself to slip into her thoughts and disappear. But that was how it had always been when she got in the zone—especially while cooking. She glanced in his direction but didn't say a word.

"Do you want to talk about it?"

Holding her breath so she didn't let out the sigh she knew hovered, waiting to be released, Ava shook her head.

"You sure? Because I feel like you really want to—"

No longer able to contain it, she blew out a harsh breath through pursed lips. "Want to *what*, Max? Want to talk about how you've done all this great stuff and you're not even thirty yet? Or how about the fact that I'm still living with my grandmother when I should be out on my own making a life for myself? Not everyone can be as *amazing* as you." Her eyes widened and she clapped a hand over her mouth. She hadn't meant to say any of that.

In fact, she wasn't even sure where those thoughts had come from. She wasn't jealous of Max. On the contrary, she was proud of him for everything he was doing to change the world. Ava didn't understand why he needed a flashy car and other showy trappings of his wealth but that was his choice. So why did it feel like they weren't equals anymore?

Because they weren't.

Nothing had been made clearer than that exact point from the moment she'd walked back into his life. Into his ritzy office, where she was delivering his coffee, for Pete's sake.

Max had everything figured out. He knew what he wanted out of his life and he knew how to get it.

It was hard to think back to when they were younger and remember much, but she did know one thing. Max had wanted to be a father. Did he still dream of having his own family, or had life made him too bitter?

"Ava," his voice echoed through her reverie, dragging her from the endless ocean of intruding thoughts and she glanced at him again.

"What?" she muttered, suddenly realizing she was blushing. Great. Now he knew she was bothered about her job, the differences in their lives and that she couldn't keep her big mouth shut. What else could go wrong?

"Is that what you think?" He moved closer to her. His hands came down on her shoulders and he forced her to face him. He wasn't much taller than she was, but there was enough of a difference she needed to lift her chin a bit to gaze directly into his eyes.

And what she saw there made her stomach churn. Why did he have to have the most discerning gaze she'd seen in her lifetime? This was why she'd never been able to keep secrets from him. It all made sense now.

He continued. "You can't possibly think that my life is perfect."

She snorted. "Okay, you're right. No one's life is perfect but yours comes pretty darn close. Am I going to find some genie's lamp at your place?"

When the corners of his mouth twitched, the tightness in her chest seemed to ease, even if it was only a little bit. "Come on, Ava. I'm being serious."

Poking him firmly enough in the chest that he grunted, she forced her voice to lighten up. "That's your problem. You're always too serious."

"No, I'm not."

She crossed her arms and gave him a pointed look. "Are too. Always have been and always will be."

"Take that back," he muttered.

"See?" she laughed. "You can't even have a conversation with me, without getting defensive." Yes, she could see the irony. She'd been the grumpy one not even two minutes ago. Normally, she would have allowed herself to wallow a little, but she couldn't afford to do that, not with Max here.

Unexpectedly, he turned, his focus sweeping the kitchen.

What was he looking for? Did he think there would be some kind of proof that he wasn't a stick in the mud?

"It's okay, Max. I still like you even if you—" White powder flew through the air, clouding the space around her head and getting into her mouth. Ava coughed, waving her hand in front of her face. "Did you just throw flour at me?" She coughed again. "You can't seriously think that would make a difference." Blinking, she attempted to wipe whatever she could from her cheeks before fixing a stern glare on him. "That was highly inappropriate."

This was the moment when Max should have been smug. He should have been laughing that he'd gotten her. But he was just as serious as ever. "*See*?" He muttered. "I can be fun."

Ava stared at him in disbelief. "You think you're being *fun*?" She gestured around her where specks of white covered her clothes, the counter, and the floor. "This isn't fun. This is a mess."

"Same thing."

Her mouth fell open. "You're serious."

"No. That is the opposite of what I'm trying to prove."

Without considering what the consequences could be, she charged for the sink and grabbed the spraying wand. Max's eyes widened and he held up his hands. "Now Ava, think about what you're doing."

"I am thinking about what I'm doing. I'm going to clean up."

He shook his head. "That's only going to make the mess worse."

"You should have thought about that before you—" More flour rained down around her and she gasped. "You *didn't*."

Max chuckled.

Before he could say anything or do anything to stop her, she held down the trigger and water shot out of the wand. She hadn't bothered turning it to the warmer temperature, he needed to know her wrath—but there was one problem. The cord connected to the wand could only go so far and when Max darted away from her, all she accomplished was a wet floor.

"Get back here," she demanded.

He was pressed up against the farthest wall from the sink, not a speck of flour on him, nor a drip of water. He shook his head, a hint of a smile gracing his handsome face. "I'm not coming anywhere near you while you're wielding that weapon."

"None of this would have happened if you hadn't thrown flour at my face."

"At least you still look cute. If you sprayed me, I'd look like a drowned rat."

She snorted. "You still deserve to get some payback."

"That may be, but I'm going to have to take a rain check."

Ava rolled her eyes. "Very funny."

"Now you get it: I can be funny."

"That wasn't the argument. I said you weren't any *fun*." The whole time they were having this argument, the wheels in her head were turning. If she could fill up a cup of water, she might be able to surprise him and exact her vengeance.

But there was one problem.

Ava had a propensity for being easily distracted.

Max had inched close enough that when she wasn't paying attention, he charged forward so both of their hands held the wand. His voice lowered as he spoke close to her ear. "Checkmate."

Goose bumps rose on her arms. She couldn't tell if it was from his proximity, or from the cool water that had sprayed back on her when she'd attempted to douse him. Either way, the sensation wasn't something she wanted to continue.

Max pried the wand from her hand, leaving her defenseless. She had one shot to make this work. There was a forgotten plastic cup in the sink. It wasn't the best plan, but it was all she had. She darted for the handle on the sink faucet, flipping it on. It filled the cup for a brief moment until Max realized what her plans were. He aimed the wand at her.

It was like everything slowed down. Ava grabbed the cup and spun around to fling it at Max just as he held down the trigger of the water sprayer.

At the exact same moment that the water from her cup splashed Max in the face, she was sprayed with a dose of the same chilled water.

Ava squealed, darting away from Max and giving him the upper hand. She hid around the side of the refrigerator. "How dare you!"

"How dare *I*? How dare *you*. You're the one who started this."

"Because you're *no fun*."

"Not that again," he groaned exaggeratedly which only caused a string of giggles to escape her throat. "You want *no fun*? Then come a little closer and I'll show you *no fun*."

"Nah, I think I'm good over here."

"What about the cookies?"

"I think you can take care of those all on your own."

Max stared forlornly at the countertop where all the ingredients had been set out. "But you promised." If it weren't for the fact that he still held the sprayer, she might have given in and returned to her station. But she knew this was all a ploy. She was smarter than that. He glanced at her again, holding up the sprayer with his fingers no longer wrapped around the handle. "Okay, let's call a truce."

Ava shook her head. "I can't do that. Not until you give me a sign of good faith."

"Oh yeah? Like what? You want me to clean everything up?"

"That's a start."

Another sigh, which added to her joy. She'd forgotten how much she'd loved spending time with him. "What else?"

"Self-sabotage."

"What does that even mean?"

She laughed. "Spray yourself. Make it even."

"Spray my—" he shook his head. "I can't do that."

"Why not?"

He made a big show of holding out his arms and turning side to side. "Do you know how expensive this suit is?" Max probably hadn't meant to do it, but he'd once again emphasized their differences. He had money and power. And she had ... nothing—nothing but her grandmother.

She shoved those dismal thoughts aside, crossing her arms as she did so like the action would protect her from the thoughts returning. "Your suit is already wet. If water ruins it, then it's long gone. Level the playing field, Max. Show me that it doesn't matter. That's what you wanted to tell me earlier, right? Money? Social status? None of it matters and if that's true, then you'll prove it." The words came from her mouth before she had a chance to analyze them.

But when she did, she immediately regretted bringing their socioeconomic status into the conversation. Before she could withdraw her statement, Max had turned the spray nozzle toward himself.

Ava held up her hands, but it was too late.

Max held down the nozzle and the water poured down his head, shoulders, and the rest of his body.

She gasped, her hand covering her mouth to stop the laughter from escaping. He actually did it. Max actually ruined a suit for her.

Okay, not for her.

He did it for cookies.

"Max," she whispered. "What were you thinking?"

A look of pure betrayal crossed his face. "You told me to."

"Yeah, and if I told you to jump off a bridge, would you do it?" She'd pushed his easygoing nature too far on that one. The sprayer clattered into the sink as Max charged toward her like a bull chasing the matador.

She shrieked, darting around the island and then weaving behind the kitchen table, but he was too fast. His hands wrapped around her waist, capturing her before he turned her around and pulled her close.

Ava threw her head back and laughed as she pressed her hands against his chest. "You're soaked! Ugh! Max, stop it!"

He laughed along with her, a sound she hadn't heard since they were in high school. "You're getting every last second of this hug. First of all, it's way overdue, and second, you deserve to be just as cold and wet as me."

It didn't matter how much she squirmed, there was no escaping Max's hold on her.

"Is everything all right? I heard screaming." Rosalie's voice called from the hall.

Saved by the interruption, Ava pulled back. She had to cover her mouth with her hand to prevent herself from laughing too loudly.

Max glanced at her, then over his shoulder. "Everything's fine. Just spilled a little water. We're cleaning it up now."

There wasn't any further comment from Rosalie, and the only sound in the kitchen was their heavy breathing.

Ava giggled again. "You're terrible."

"That's better than being boring." Max grinned at her. "As long as I'm fun, I don't care."

Chapter Nine

Max watched with interest as Ava set to work making the batter for the macarons. It was fluffy like whipped cream at one point, and then a little more liquid toward the end. Ava had a talent for piping the batter into circles that all looked exactly the same.

He didn't know if he would have ever been able to do something like that.

Okay, he *definitely* knew he wouldn't be able to.

People who could create desserts like this were born to do it, which begged the question: why did Ava avoid discussing it at all costs?

She'd rather have an argument about nonsense than talk about her future. He glanced up at her while she worked, noting the cute way she stuck out her tongue when she was focusing very hard.

Her eyes darted over to meet his and she smiled. "What?"

"I'm just thinking."

"What about?" she put down her piping bag and wiped the back of her wrist against her forehead.

"I'm curious why you're trying so hard to avoid talking about opening a bakery."

Immediately, the smile faded from her face. "Because I don't want to be a baker."

"Liar."

She turned a hard gaze on him. "I beg your pardon?"

"You heard me just fine. You want to be a baker. You've always wanted it. Have you forgotten that I know you better than you know yourself?"

Ava folded her arms, her lips pressed into a thin line. Either she was too upset to speak to him or she was worried she'd hurt him by spewing what she really felt in this moment. "You *knew* me better than I knew myself." Turned out, she wasn't too shy to tell him after all.

"Fine. We don't know each other as well as we used to. But I can tell that baking still brings you joy. I've just seen it with my own eyes. Your nana sees it too. So why are you so dead set against it?"

This time her eyes darted away. She shifted beneath his stare. If she'd had any escape route, she would have taken it.

"What happened to the girl who wasn't scared of anything?"

She shot him a sharp look. "I'm not scared."

"Then prove it."

"I don't need to prove anything to you."

He climbed off the stool and wandered around the island. "You're right. You don't have to prove anything to me. But you do have to prove it to yourself. If you spend the rest of your life doing something you don't love, then you're going to spend just as much time wondering *what if?* What if you took a chance on something exhilarating and new? What is the worst thing that could happen?"

"They won't like it," she blurted, then her eyes dropped

down to her wringing hands. "What if they try what I've made and they don't like it? What if they call me a fraud or something equally depressing?"

The Ava he'd known would have never brought up these kinds of concerns. She'd been fearless from the moment he'd met her. Max didn't know when this change happened, but he wasn't going to sit by and let it continue to get in her way. Maybe *this* was the reason they wandered into one another's lives again.

He was here to help her realize her dreams.

"Cater my charity event," he blurted it before he knew what he was saying. It was like his head had decided to hand the reins over to his heart and let his heart make all the crazy decisions. Max should just take it back. She had said herself she wasn't interested. She'd pushed back against that idea more than once, but he couldn't bring himself to tell her she was right to do so. There had to be a reason Ava was brought back into his life, and it wasn't so he could force her to break up with her boyfriend, nor rekindle whatever this was that seemed to have sparked between them.

He needed to help her get back on track to who she'd wanted to be all along.

In this very moment, the way she was staring at him made him feel especially sheepish. He'd demanded something from her after agreeing to let her think it over and it hadn't even been an hour. The anxiety in her gaze had completely disappeared, but it hadn't been replaced with anything he could read. She crossed her arms, and continued to drill her focus into him until he couldn't stand it anymore. "Well? Are you going to put me out of my misery and say you'll do it? I'm sure your nana would be with me on this."

"I already know the two of you have probably been planning this from the very beginning."

He snorted. "Seriously? You believe I have the kind of time to come over here, have a chat with Rosalie and tell her to nudge you in the right direction?"

"Nudge? More like shove me off a cliff. Neither of you are willing to let me come to terms with this idea. It's a little exhausting."

"Good."

Ava's brows shot up. "What?"

"If you're uncomfortable, then we're pushing you out of that comfort zone."

"Maybe I like my comfort zone. Have you ever thought of that?" Her face was flushed and her breathing had grown shallow. "Maybe I don't want to risk it all and end up falling flat on my face. I don't have the luxury you do, Max. I can't just throw money at something and be okay if I end up being wrong about the whole thing."

"Wow. We're going to revisit that later." She had a lot more hang-ups about money than he'd realized. If that was where all these problems were rooted, then he'd make her an offer she wouldn't be able to refuse. He closed the distance between them and pried her hands from her folded arms. She didn't look up at him, but rather kept her eyes lowered beneath her scowl. Max itched to lift her chin, to force her to meet his gaze so she would get the full weight of what he was about to tell her. But he didn't. He'd already pushed her a little too far. "When I ask you to cater my event, I'm not doing it out of charity. You'd be worth every single penny I pay you."

Still she didn't look at him.

"Ava, nothing great in this life will be worth having if you find it in your comfort zone. Nothing," he repeated. "Anything of value ... you have to step outside of that protective bubble and take it before someone else does."

Slowly, she lifted her chin.

"I can think of no one better to ask than you. This could be your debut."

"I don't want to fail," she whispered.

"If you fail?" He shrugged. "Then you still get paid, and you can return to the coffee shop gig you love so much. But let me ask you one thing." He touched his forehead to hers, his voice lowering to a whisper. "What if you don't?"

They stood like that in the quiet kitchen, holding hands and heads barely touching for several minutes. He wasn't sure where her heart was at. She gave no clues to which way she was leaning. The temptation to give her a gentle shake to put some sense into her head was so strong he ended up holding onto her hands a little tighter.

Finally she blew out a painfully slow breath. "Fine."

He stiffened, his eyes widening. "Fine?"

She tore away from him, letting out a groan. "I said okay, all right? I'll do it."

He let out a loud roar, shooting his fists into the air as he leaped along with it.

Ava spun to face him with surprise. Her pointer finger pressed to her lips as she shook her head. "Shh! Nana is trying to sleep!"

Max ducked his head and chuckled. "To be fair, I think she would probably be just as excited as I am about this."

"Yeah, maybe." She glanced toward the stairs. "Okay, most definitely. But that doesn't mean you need to get her out of bed again. I can tell her in the morning."

"I'm just glad you finally agreed. I can send Peter a message and let him know the desserts are covered."

Ava picked up her piping bag again, and her voice shifted to something more nonchalant. "I really hope you're not paying him too much."

He paused, his phone already in hand. "What is that supposed to mean?"

She didn't even miss a beat. "Because if you're going to have me, it's gonna cost you a pretty penny."

His mouth quirked upward into a half-smile. "Oh yeah? How much is this going to set me back?"

This time she glanced at him, unable to hide the smile that touched her lips. "I dunno. I was thinking that perhaps I should get enough for a down payment."

Max glanced around the house where she currently lived. It was nice enough and her nana was probably incredibly grateful to have her granddaughter staying with her. "You want to move?"

She frowned. "What? No, where did you get that idea?"

"You said you wanted enough for a down payment."

Understanding flooded her features and her smile returned. "No, dummy. I need a down payment for a bakery. If I'm going to seize the day and all that, then I'm going to need a place to do it, right?"

"Really?" He couldn't deny the excitement that flooded his entire being. This was what he'd been saying all along. "You're seriously going to consider it? Ava, that's great. You're going to be so good at it—"

She slapped the piping bag onto the palm of her other hand. "Okay, okay. I was mostly teasing about that. Clearly, I'm not worth that much—"

"How much do you believe I think my caterers are worth? If I say you're going to get paid a certain amount, then I'm going to fulfill my end of the bargain. You just worry about putting together a menu."

"Max, you can't be serious—"

He picked up his phone and placed it to his ear right after tapping Peter's contact information. His grin spread ear to ear as he held his finger in the air to cut her off. It was one of his favorite ways to get what he wanted with people who worked with him, and he wasn't above using it with Ava.

She scoffed, her eyes following him as he headed out of the kitchen and into the sitting room. The phone rang and rang until voicemail picked up.

"Hey Peter, it's Maximus. I've got some good news for you. There's someone else I've hired to do the dessert menu. You're going to love her. I think that will solve your problem of trying to get it all done single-handedly. Give me a call when you get this message and we'll talk details." He hung up the phone and released a pent-up breath. If there was one thing he could do to make the world a little better and a little brighter, it was to help Ava Brooks find her calling.

And if she was too busy to spend time with him, perhaps he'd be able to get his mind off the girl he'd pined far too long for.

Max shoved his phone into his pocket and headed back into the kitchen. Once again, Ava was hard at work, her little tongue sticking out as she focused on the details of the cookie she currently worked on.

He snatched one from the tray and she jumped, her hand darting out to rescue it. "You can't eat it until it dries."

Max's face scrunched up with confusion. "The frosting has to dry?"

"Yes. Otherwise it's just going to be a runny mess." She laughed.

"What if I want to live on the dangerous side?" He eyed another cookie.

"Don't you even think about it," she laughed again, but this time she aimed her frosting bag at him. "I've got a weapon and I know how to use it."

He shook his head. "Have you forgotten so soon how this will turn out for you?" He glanced toward the sink and she followed his gaze, giving him just long enough of a distraction for him to grab a cookie that she'd just completed.

THE COOKIE MATCH

She turned just in time to see him take a small bite, only for a dribble of unset frosting to land on his front.

He made a strangled sound, but it was easily overtaken by her laughter. "You really should listen to me, you know."

Max wiped at his chin then licked his fingers. "Yeah, I'm beginning to see the appeal."

Chapter Ten

"I can't believe I'm doing this. I can't believe I'm doing this. I really shouldn't be doing this." Ava paced in front of her friend's couch. But Izzie only stared up at her with amusement.

"I think it's great and I can't believe you didn't do it sooner."

Ava shot her a disgruntled look. "Not you too."

Izzie snickered. "What? Is there a support group for people who want to support Ava but she won't let them?"

She couldn't roll her eyes hard enough to show her distaste for that statement. Ava plopped herself down beside her friend and groaned. "It's like everyone decided to have an intervention, but didn't invite me until they'd made all my decisions for me."

"Now you're being ridiculous." Izzie settled back into her seat and eyed Ava with that look—the one that said she knew better and Ava might as well accept her fate.

Ava always hated that look.

"Look, it's not like everyone is going to force you to open a bakery. We just want you to give this a try. If it works out, then great. If it doesn't, then you didn't risk anything."

"You guys don't get it. This is one of the biggest risks ever. Have you seen the kind of people who go to these things? They're rich. Like *really* rich."

Izzie lifted a brow. "You make that sound like a bad thing."

Ava sighed. "You know what I mean. Come on, your Bart doesn't really count anyway. He wasn't born rich."

"According to you, neither was Max."

"Oh, hush," Ava muttered. "The people at this event are going to be super wealthy folk from all over the country. I wonder if some of them come to these things only to make themselves look good, and feel good, after they throw money at a charity."

"Is that really how you feel about them?" There was a distinctly hurt tone in Izzie's voice, one that caught Ava completely off guard.

She sat up a little straighter. "I didn't mean it like that."

"How exactly did you mean it? It isn't fair to lump people together based on their bank balance. And I still don't see how this is going to be such a bad thing. Really, Ava. You keep coming up with reasons that no one believes, because they're unbelievable. I know you as such a confident person. Aren't you willing to give this a go?"

Slumping back into her seat, Ava shrugged. "I don't know. I thought I did, but I'm just not sure anymore. It's like the second Max and my paths crossed, things changed."

"You ... think ... this has something to do with Max?"

Ava dug her hands into her hair. "No. Of course not ..." Then she peeked at her friend. "Maybe? I don't know. Everything was going ... fine. And then I took him that coffee and it was like the world shifted. I can't explain it."

"Do you ... like him?"

She shot a sharp look in Izzie's direction. "No. Definitely not."

Izzie's pointed stare suggested she didn't believe that statement for a second.

"Even if I was on the market, it would never work out."

"Why's that?"

"Because ... he's Maximus Stone, that's why. A million woman would gladly throw themselves at his feet for just one date. He's the most eligible bachelor in the area. Maybe in the state."

"So?"

"*So?*" Ava groaned. "So, he's not my type and we're friends. That's all it ever was and that is all it will ever be. Besides, I told you. I'm swearing off relationships because so far I've never met a guy who turns out to be anything like what they show you at first."

Izzie laughed this time. "You make it sound like you can just go to the grocery store and pick out a guy like you would a pineapple."

"Well, that's how it should be, don't you think? At least then you can smell them and pick the right one."

More laughter. "Firstly, ew. And secondly, you sound so jaded."

"No, I'm just over it. And now I'm stuck catering this event, when I have no idea what I'm doing."

Her friend reached out and touched her arm gently. "You're going to do great. We all know it. You're a wiz in the kitchen. The people at the charity auction won't know what hit their taste buds when you're done with them. I guarantee it."

Ava offered her a small smile. "You're just saying that because you're my friend."

"Nope." Izzie leaned back in her seat and crossed her arms as if to drive home her next statement. "I'm saying it because I don't want you to forget me when you become this famous baker. Because one day people will line the street just to get a taste of those cookies you make and I'm going to want to call in a favor so you can put me at the front of the line."

There was no fighting the smile that spread across her face. Ava leaned over and gave her friend a hug. "I can always count on you to bring me back to reality. I don't know what I would do without you."

"I know," Izzie said simply and then she laughed. "But seriously. You better not make me wait in the back of the line. You know how much I've grown accustomed to *being rich*." She said it with a dramatic flair to which Ava laughed again.

❋

"I know this isn't what you're accustomed to, but I figured I'd offer the use of the kitchen to you until we get set up at the venue." Peter led Ava through the doors into the kitchen at Maple Gardens.

Her eyes bounced and ricocheted from the stainless-steel countertops to the pots and pans hanging on one wall. This wasn't anything like she'd been expecting from a retirement community.

"I hope it's okay." Peter murmured, also taking it all in.

"Okay? This place is amazing. I can't believe the owner would let you use this place for something that isn't even benefiting Maple Gardens."

Peter glanced at her out of the corner of his eye. "Lily has been here for a while. I'd wager either she or Maximus called in a few favors to make this happen."

"I'm beginning to realize that Max usually gets what he wants," she murmured. It wouldn't surprise her; he'd gotten her to agree to help with the catering.

"Hmm?"

Her eyes cut to Peter's. "Nothing." She smiled at him. "This will be great. I'm just worried I'm going to be stepping on your toes. You have a community to cook for. I can't just take over the kitchen with my menu planning."

"Oh, you're not going to step on his toes at all. He's used to people being underfoot."

Ava turned to find a familiar young woman looping her arm through Peter's. She winked at Ava. "Hi. I'm Quinne."

Quinne. The name seemed to tickle at a memory in the back of her mind. Where had she heard that name before. Knowing her, it was a name she'd written on a hundred paper cups at the coffee shop. That's probably where she knew this woman from.

"I'm *not* used to people being underfoot. You're just underfoot all the time."

She kissed him on the cheek. "And you love it."

"Correction: I love *you*," he muttered. His eyes swung back to Ava. "But I'm sure you'll be just fine. The only issue we might run into is refrigerator space. I like to keep a lot of fresh food on hand for the residents. It's better than the frozen or canned stuff."

"I couldn't agree more." She nodded toward a large metal door. "Is that it? It looks like a walk-in."

"It is. We just got an upgrade last week."

Quinne scoffed. "You've only had it a week and you don't think you can accommodate her stuff? What are you filling it with? Gold bars?"

Peter rolled his eyes. "I'll see what I can do to move things around a little—"

Ava waved her hands. "Don't worry about it. I'm not going to be needing a lot of space. I might not even be here that often. I have to try out a few recipes before I know what I'm going to make. The issue will be figuring out how to scale them up for a large group."

"Well, that's perfect then." Quinne beamed, her gaze shifting from Ava to Peter. "The residents here would love to have a special treat every so often. I'd bet that Isaac would even approve something like that in the budget."

"Isaac?"

"Isaac Spencer owns this place. He'd be the one to oversee something like that," Peter confirmed. "But Quinne is right. If you want to scale up a recipe, the folks here love sweets more than just about anything."

"Who doesn't?" Quinne laughed then nudged Peter. "Remember when I let them help me cook a few things? They were always wanting to make something sweet."

That's when Ava realized where she recognized Quinne from. "You're the one who put out all of those videos about cooking with grandparents or something like that."

Quinne chuckled. "Yeah, that's me. Isaac wants me to do some more stuff like that for his expansion. Not sure what it's going to entail, but it sounds fun."

"That's amazing! I've always been so impressed that you've been able to get out there and do what you love and get paid to do it. You don't understand how much people like me look up to people like you."

"You're so sweet. But really, it doesn't take much, except to be enthusiastic about what you love to do. People feed off it, you know?"

Ava shook her head. "It's so much more than that. The world is saturated with people who create their own content or start their own business and a lot have a hard time staying above water. I don't think I could ever do what you do."

"Everyone starts somewhere."

"She's right, you know." Peter's voice broke into their conversation. "You're not going to get anywhere if you don't start from somewhere."

The women exchanged glances, then Quinne giggled.

"What?" he murmured.

Quinne turned to Ava. "I'm finally rubbing off on him. He used to be holed up in this kitchen day in and day out."

"I happen to like being holed up in this kitchen."

"Yeah," Quinne drawled, "but now you get to branch out and get some recognition. You deserve every bit of fame that brings you."

He made a face. "I don't want fame. Definitely not like the fame you have."

Ava watched the two bicker with interest. They were clearly so much in love, but their relationship was also rooted firmly in their friendship. It was hard to see where one stopped and the other began. She hadn't had anything like this with Kevin. The only male friendship she had at this point was her rekindled one with Max, and he was not going to become anything more.

Not even if she was remotely curious.

Because she wasn't.

Right?

Ava pushed down those treacherous thoughts and nodded toward the door. "Thanks for the tour. I'll let you know when I'm ready to set up shop. For now, I need to get to work. I'm already late as it is."

The couple waved her out the door and she headed for her car. Quinne had a way of infusing the people around her with a light and a drive that Ava hadn't felt since she was younger. It was strange being in her presence and realizing that everything she'd ever wanted, which had always seemed just out of reach, was inching closer and closer. Could she actually make this work? If she made a splash on her first try, didn't she owe it to herself to jump in with eyes shut tight?

Because that was exactly what she wanted to do.

And it was all Max's fault.

Chapter Eleven

Max stared out the window of his office, unable to concentrate. The whole day was practically wasted and it was all because he couldn't get that one night out of his head. The night he'd gone to Ava's home and pushed her to realize her dreams were attainable.

All it had taken was a few hours with her and his feelings had come rushing back. He'd forgotten how much he loved being with her. Forgotten how easy it was to tease her—and be teased by her. And how much it mattered that she had opportunities the way he had. Since that night, he'd told himself to keep his distance. He didn't need to get hung up on a girl who had zero interest in dating him. That was the first thing he needed to accept. The second was that he didn't want to ruin the friendship he'd rediscovered, and if he spent *too* much time with her he might do just that.

His pacing quickened. Ava wasn't the issue he needed to be concerning himself with at the moment. There were several work-related things he needed to wrap up before he could really dive deep into this charity event.

If the event didn't go well, he'd only have himself to

blame. Ava needed this even more than he did. He was determined to make sure that Ava would come out on top. He'd hired her to do the catering. He'd already found a nice kitchen for her to use. Was there anything else he could do?

"Mr. Stone? You have a delivery."

He jumped, spinning around to face his secretary as she stood in the half-opened doorway. She eyed him as if she were unsure whether or not she should bring it to him. "Well, what is it?"

"She ..." Cathy nibbled on her lower lip before she glanced over her shoulder then swung her gaze back to him. She lowered her voice, "She won't let me bring it to you."

"Who is it?"

"It's that coffee lady again. I told her it's policy for deliveries to be left at my—"

His stomach lurched. "Let her in."

"But sir—"

"I said let her in. She's my friend. She doesn't need to follow the same guidelines I have in place for basic deliveries."

Cathy sighed and retreated from the doorway. Moments later, Ava appeared with two cups. She glanced back, presumably toward his secretary, then shut the door. "Boy, that secretary of yours has an attitude, doesn't she?"

"She's not so bad once you get to know her." Max remained by the window, his hands behind his back.

"I think she likes you."

Max chuckled. "You don't know her like I do. That's just how she is. She's very protective."

Ava lifted a brow. "I don't know ... she really didn't want me bringing you your coffee."

He glanced down at the drinks. "You know I have a coffee machine here, right? You didn't have to get me coffee."

She frowned. "I ... didn't. This was another order with specific instructions ..."

He smacked his forehead with his palm. "*Quinne*! I swear if she keeps pulling this stuff, I'm really going to consider rescinding her invitation to the charity gala."

"Quinne? As in Quinne Hart?" Ava placed the coffees on the desk. "I just met her today. You think she's doing this?"

"You met her? Did she say anything about me?"

Ava's confused expression would have been hilarious if it wasn't so genuine. "I don't think Quinne is the one treating you to coffee. She's dating someone else."

"She's engaged to someone else."

Ava's brows shot up. "Well then, I really don't think she's treating you to coffee. This has to be from someone else."

"No. You don't get it," he sighed. "Her mother is friends with my mother at Maple Gardens. A little while back, a group of them fancied themselves matchmakers and set up Bartholomew Brown with a young woman whose mother lives there. It's a convoluted story—"

"You mean Izzie?" Ava blinked a few times. "You think that Quinne set up Izzie and Bart? Because I can assure you—"

"No. It was Isaac's mother, my mother and Quinne's mother."

Ava shook her head. "Okay. You lost me. What does this have to do with Quinne buying you coffee and Izzie falling for Bart?"

He stared at her, unable to form the words that would make any lick of sense. "Like I said, it's convoluted. Just trust me. Quinne's in on it because my mother knows better than to mess with my life. But Quinne met Peter through them, and people talk. I'm sure this has something to do with it."

She laughed. "You sorta sound like a conspiracy theorist."

"It's not a conspiracy. They're making it their mission to pair off all of the unmarried folks who visit."

"Okay, buddy. Remind me to get you a tinfoil hat." She

picked up the cups and turned them around, then her brows furrowed. "This one has my name on it."

He froze then hurried forward to grab the cup. Sure enough, her name was scrawled across the order sticker. "Did you seriously not realize you were writing your own name?"

"I didn't make the order. But this is weirding me out."

Max gestured toward the cup. "No tinfoil needed."

"Fine, then it's a joke. They're toying with you." She shoved the cup into his chest. "Just laugh along with them and don't let it bother you. Then they'll leave you alone."

"They're doing this because they want us to get together for some reason."

"Now I know you're being ridiculous. They're teasing you. The last time you visited your mother, did I even come up?" Ava picked up the cup with her name and took a sip.

"What? Of course not. I don't talk about you at all." The second the words slipped from his lips he regretted them. Heat slithered up his neck and into his face, making it difficult to maintain eye contact. He lowered his voice a bit and looked away. "But my mom knows you're one of the reasons I hated the decision she made. I lost a lot when we moved. And your friendship was at the top of the list."

"Well, that's it then. She probably mentioned something to the other women. And Quinne wanted to be on the other side of things. Makes sense."

"It's not up to them who I date."

She groaned exaggeratedly and moved across the room to take a seat. Plopping onto an overstuffed chair, she gave him a pointed look. "It's not like they set us up on a blind date or even a double date. They're not forcing you to start a relationship with me. At best, they're just making sure we're back in each other's lives. And guess what? They succeeded. I for one am grateful."

He worked his jaw, contemplating what she was saying.

Ava was right. They might be pushing him toward her, but that didn't mean anything would happen.

No.

He wasn't going to go there. He wanted a friendship. That was it. Max grabbed his coffee and wandered toward her, then sat perched on the armrest of the chair where she sat. He took a sip of his drink and let out a sigh. "You're probably right."

"Oh, I'm definitely right. And hey, if it means I'm going to be forced to bring you coffee a few times a week and neither one of us has to pay for it, then so be it." She craned her neck around so she could gaze up at him.

His pulse accelerated as he stared down into her blue eyes. They were the same color as the sky on a summer afternoon or pools of clear ocean water that he could drown in. For a moment it felt like she was feeling something similar—her focus grew distant and her smile faded. But then she blinked and edged a few inches to the other side of the chair. "I took a tour of the kitchen at Maple Gardens today. It's really nice. I can't believe they have a setup like that at a retirement community."

"The guy who started the place actually lives there. He's elderly now and has some health issues."

"Then he's lucky he had the money to make his future so comfortable." There was a sadness about Ava's words. "Other people don't get that. Like Nana."

"But not everything is about money."

"Well, sometimes it feels like it is.

She stood up, placed her coffee cup on a nearby table and flashed him a tired smile. "I should probably get back to work."

Max shot to his feet. "Ava—" He strode after her.

"See you around, Max. Maybe tomorrow, maybe in a week. Who knows when these little matchmakers will strike next?"

Before he could reach her, she'd slipped out the door.

Man, she was fast. And it wasn't like he could chase her down. The last thing he needed was for anyone on his floor to see him charging after the coffee delivery woman. They would most definitely get the wrong idea.

No, he wasn't angry about her service.

And no, he wasn't dating her.

Though, that last one wouldn't be so bad, if he didn't feel like there was a chasm the size of the Grand Canyon between them.

Max stood in the doorway of his office and watched her across the large lobby, where she stood at the elevator pressing the button several times. He was tempted to call out to her that pushing it like that wouldn't make the elevator come any faster, but doing so would be as bad as chasing her out of his office.

So instead, he watched her disappear, wondering why she couldn't just accept that the money he had wasn't something he had any choice over. It was all he had as a connection to his father and surely he should get some credit for all the good he was doing with that money?

How was he supposed to explain that to her without sounding like the pompous jerk she already thought him to be?

He released a sigh and retreated into his office. Placing the coffee cup on the edge of his desk, he stopped and stared out the window. There was nothing he could do to bridge this gap.

Unless there was.

Ava thought the thing that separated them was money. But what if he removed that from the equation? What if he could come up with a way to show her that money wasn't an issue for him? Then maybe she'd let her guard down just a little more when she was around him.

THE COOKIE MATCH

He snapped his fingers, already formulating a plan in his head. Ava was going to love it. Well, the old Ava would have loved it. This new one might be a bit trickier.

Max spun around to face his desk, then yanked out a lined piece of paper. At the top of the page he wrote, *Come up with some free stuff to impress Ava.*

Because, well, money wasn't everything.

Chapter Twelve

With each step Ava took to get back to the coffee shop, she grew more agitated.

She wasn't so prejudiced that she believed everyone who had money was inherently evil. But even Max had to admit that when people didn't have to worry about finances, they acted differently. They were more frivolous with their spending and that bled into the way they treated others.

But then there were people like Max.

He was still the best friend who'd made her laugh and dream bigger than the sky. Before he left her to embrace his wonderful new life.

Ava marched into the coffee shop and her friend behind the counter smiled brightly at her. "How did it go?"

"Fine," she muttered. "Except someone is trying to match us up and I don't want any more of being sent to deliver coffees because someone thinks it funny to play with our lives."

Trina shot her a confused look. "You didn't know the coffees were ordered for you both?"

"Not until I noticed my name."

"I had no idea, Ava. Sorry."

"Not your fault. I just don't understand why anyone would try and get us together. We're not who we used to be. Actually, I am, but Max is..."

"Go on."

"It's not that I hate people who have more money than me. I know it's what makes the world go round. I get it, I do. But when I pointed out how we were basically two people from different worlds, he just ... I dunno, gave me this *look*." Ava's voice trailed off and her heart sank a little lower. "It was like he thought I was talking about him."

"To be fair, when you generalize like that, it never turns out right. It's like this thing you have with your new no-relationship policy. Not all men are bad. Look at Ryan. He and I have been together for a couple years."

"But Ryan is actually a good one." Ava pointed out.

"And there are others out there. If you're going to push away every man who might try to get close to you, then what's going to happen when the first good one tries to make his move and you turn him down flat?"

Ava huffed. "What is it with you two? It's like you guys are taking pleasure in putting me in my place."

Trina beamed. "It's all part of the job."

"So, what are you saying? I should go apologize for generalizing? That's not a crime."

"No, but he might have taken offense at it. Didn't you say he was given his money later in life? How much do you want to bet that he still identifies as that kid who grew up with nothing."

Trina's words hit Ava in the gut, hard. She'd put up this wall between herself and her childhood friend all because he'd gotten money. It hadn't been intentional, but somewhere beneath the surface, she had been keeping him at arm's length. If only he hadn't ghosted her after that first phone call. Had they stayed in touch she could have celebrated his successes over the years instead of feeling... left out.

Ava sighed. "Yeah. You're probably right."

"Oh, I know I'm right. Just like I know I'm right when I give you this." She held out a small slip of paper and grinned.

Ava took it as her gaze drilled into her friend's with suspicion. When she dropped her gaze to the paper, she found a phone number scrawled across it. She rolled her eyes and held the paper out toward her friend. "No."

"No?" Trina laughed. "What are you talking about?"

"I'm not taking this. I'm not calling whoever this Dalton guy is, and I'm not going on a date."

"No one ever said anything about going on a date. You served him this morning before you took off to make the delivery. He didn't get a chance to ask you for your number, so he asked if I would give this to you."

"Like I said: No."

"You can't swear off men forever, you know."

"But I can certainly try," Ava said with a smile. "Besides, when would I have the time? I'm basically doing two jobs now. This and that catering thing. I have to plan a menu and experiment with a few different things before I can confidently serve the hundreds, if not thousands, of people that Max invites to these things." She shook the little scrap of paper at her friend again.

Trina glanced at the phone number then shook her head. "I'm not taking it back. If you don't want to call him, you decide what you're gonna do with it. Out of my hands, now."

Before Ava could utter her dissent, Trina's face brightened as a customer approached. "Welcome to Just Peachy. What can I get for you?"

Ava scowled at the phone number for a moment before

marching over to the trash can. She held it over the trash, then sighed and shoved the note into her pocket. Why did Trina have to make so much sense?

Maybe her friends were right. She needed to stop generalizing the negative that she interacted with. Not all rich people were bad and not all men were either. Max was a testament to both of those statements.

❄

Ava sat in front of a glowing television screen, her notebook in her hand and the end of a pen between her teeth. Nana sat beside her, a bowl of popcorn in her lap as they watched a rerun of *Murder She Wrote*.

If she could come up with even one unique dessert, she knew she could plan the whole menu around it and she'd have it made.

The hard part was that most desserts she could think of were the traditional ones that people would expect at an event like this. Cheesecake, tarts, beignets—everything she knew she could make, but at the same time they felt boring.

Part of her wanted to just make an assortment of different cookies—choc-chip, vanilla, salted caramel—because she loved them so much. But she could add macarons ... and mini tarts that looked like cookies. Her eyes widened and she sat up straighter. Why couldn't she just do a platter of different cookies? They could all be bite-sized versions of beloved favorites, but with her own twist on things.

She scribbled down a few dessert mash-ups and her smile widened.

"You look like you've finally figured things out," her nana murmured.

When Ava glanced in her direction, she noted that Nana's eyes were still fixed on to the screen. "Yeah, I think I have."

Nana faced her, taking a piece of popcorn and popping it into her mouth. "Good. Max will be pleased."

"This isn't for Max," Ava shifted in her place on the couch, curling her legs beneath her. "This is for me. It's like you said. I need to start chasing my dreams or whatever." She didn't have to look up to know Nana was smiling at her. Of course she was. She'd been just as persistent over the years, asking Ava to take control of her life in a way that reflected the kind of potential she had.

Three sharp raps on the door drew their attention from the television. Nana placed the bowl beside her, but Ava waved her off. "I'll get it. You just try to find out who the murderer is."

"Oh, I already know. It's that doctor fella."

Ava chuckled. "Well, I suppose it *is* a rerun."

Nana's eyes twinkled. "You know my memory isn't what it used to be. I don't even remember this episode."

"Uh huh," Ava murmured with a smile. "Sure." She put her notebook down and headed for the front door. It was past seven, and most people in this neighborhood were like her grandmother. They didn't stay up late, let alone pay house calls. It was probably a food delivery guy who got lost and meant to head to the other side of town.

She opened the door and her smile faded. "Max. What are you doing here?"

He peered over her shoulder then back to her. "I hope I'm not interrupting anything."

"Who's at the door, dear?" her nana called.

"It's just Max," she answered. "I'll only be a minute."

"Max? Well, invite him in."

Ava dragged her eyes up to meet Max's, not surprised to see a smirk splitting his handsome face. Still shouting to her grandmother, she said, "I don't think he has time to stay."

"Oh, I could stay. I don't have anything going on." The grin on his face widened.

She rolled her eyes and pushed on his chest with her fingertips to prevent him from crossing the threshold. Heaven forbid Nana came searching for them. Once he was on the porch, she stepped outside and pulled the door shut behind her. "We need to talk."

"You're right. We do." His expression smoothed and he was all business. "I think we got off on the wrong foot."

"I—wait, what are you talking about?"

"After I left, we might as well have become complete strangers to one another."

"I agree," she nodded. "But—"

"And when we crossed paths again, it wasn't fair of me to expect everything to get back to the way it was before."

She didn't know where he was going with this, and she wasn't sure she wanted to. At this point, she only wanted to apologize and just let it go like water under the bridge. Unfortunately, it didn't appear that Max had the same sentiment.

"I want us to get there again—like we were before I left."

Her eyes narrowed. "Max, we can't just—"

Max held up his hand. "Hear me out. Before I left, you were my best friend. You were the one I'd tell everything to. We spent every day together just ... being us. Don't you wonder how things might have turned out if I had never left?"

She opened her mouth to answer, but he didn't let her say a word.

"Because I do." Max finally looked away, releasing her from being trapped beneath his gaze. "You're my friend. At least you used to be. And I would give anything just to have you back in my life."

Silence swallowed up his final words. A shiver tickled down her spine and back again. This was the Max she'd grown to love all those years ago—the one she'd once contemplated stealing a kiss from, before she realized just how much that would destroy what they had.

He was right. Theirs was a friendship that wasn't like anything she'd ever had before. And that was why the loss of it had hit her so hard. She swallowed hard and her question came out in a raspy whisper. "What do you have in mind?"

Chapter Thirteen

Without missing a beat, Max took hold of Ava's hand and tugged her from her front porch. Tonight was going to be all about returning to their roots. She resisted at first, but then let out a laugh and went along with him.

He stopped when they reached the sidewalk and then faced her. "I know you're an adult and all, but do you need to tell Rosalie where you're going?"

Ava shot a look over her shoulder, finding that very person standing in the window with the drapes pulled to one side. She wasn't sure but she thought she saw her grandmother wave at her. "I think she's fine with it."

"Okay, good." Max's hand tightened around hers and he hurried down the sidewalk. He passed his parked car and kept his pace quick and sure.

"Wait, where are we going? Isn't that your car?"

"We don't need it. Back in the day neither one of us had one, remember? How did we get around?" He peeked at her, relieved to see the corners of her mouth twitching.

"We walked."

"Right. Now, we're going to have to be quick if we don't want to miss out on what I have planned."

"What you have planned?" This time she did tug on him, yanking him to a stop. "What's going on, Max? This sounds like a date."

He shook his head vehemently. "This isn't a date. This is ... a girl's night out."

"You're not a girl, Max."

"I know. But you never really had any close girlfriends. I'm all you've got tonight. You just have to decide if you want to come along for the ride and have some fun."

"I don't have my purse or my phone."

"And when we were kids we didn't have that either." He jerked his chin toward the car. "I left mine behind, too. Where we're going we don't need any of that."

She shook her head and a peal of laughter escaped her lips. "You're not making any sense."

"That doesn't matter," he pulled both her hands into his. "We're getting back to our roots, Ava." He laid a serious stare on her. "Do you trust me?"

"Well, that's not really fair—"

"Do you trust me?" he repeated.

"Fine! I trust you."

"Good," he nodded, "then no more questions. Just follow me." Max took them down one street, then another, until they reached a bus stop.

When the vehicle arrived, Ava hesitated. "I don't have a bus pass. I thought you said this wouldn't cost anything."

He sighed. "Okay, so we needed a bus pass. But when we were kids, we had one. So, I've got us covered on this." He gestured toward the bus. "Your chariot awaits."

She stared at him then rolled her eyes. "I really hope I won't regret this."

Max tugged her forward and they boarded. It took about

ten minutes before they arrived at the library. Ava stared out the window and her lips curled into a smile, but she didn't say anything. They'd shared a lot of afternoons here, reading and laughing in the corner of the study room that never seemed to be used. "I wanted to bring you here so we could pick up a book."

Ava squinted at him then shook her head. "I can't believe you remembered."

"I remember everything, Ava. The years I spent with you were some of the happiest of my life." His voice had grown too serious. He could see it in the way she looked at him. Max was getting too close to revealing just how much he'd cared about her back then. He cleared his throat and flashed her a smile. "Come on. If we're fast enough we can get the next bus."

They practically ran toward the entrance of the library, which he knew was going to be closing in the next thirty minutes. He led her straight for the classics section and to the shelf he knew the book would be located. Max pulled the book from its shelf and handed it to her.

She stared down at the book then whispered, "*Great Expectations*." Her eyes flitted up to meet his. "I can't remember the last time I read this."

"I can," he murmured. "The last time I read this was when you made me."

Ava snorted.

"It's true. And I loved every minute of it." He tapped his finger on the book. "If we have time tonight, maybe we can read some of our favorite parts. But we can't right now, because we have more to do." He took the book from her, and they checked out. Then waited by the bus stop.

It was going to arrive in the next ten minutes, and with each passing second, he grew more antsy. Ava wasn't speaking to him. She'd grown abnormally quiet. Gone was the cheerful, chatty young woman he'd known, replaced with a stoic adult who had seen her share of hardship.

"Max?"

He glanced toward her.

"Why are we doing this?"

Max shrugged.

"Max," she drawled, "answer my question."

"I guess I just wanted to show you that you were wrong."

She frowned. Shoot. That wasn't what he had meant to say.

"What I mean is that you were wrong about me. I'm not any different than I was when we were close."

Ava blinked a few times, then shifted her attention to the book in her hand, tracing the letters. "I remember when I told you to read this book. I think you were complaining about how the world wasn't fair and you wished you could change things ..." Her voice trailed off.

"I'd like to think that because you made me read it, I turned out the way I did."

Her soft smile was all he needed to push him onward. He reached for her hand and gave it a gentle squeeze. "I am the man I am today because of little things like that."

She sucked in sharply then let out her breath. "That's really sweet, Max."

Before he had a chance to say anything else, the bus arrived. He motioned for her to get on first and they were off once more. This time the ride was about fifteen minutes. Ava rested her head against his shoulder as they sat beside one another. She kept the book close to her chest and still didn't say anything.

Their next stop was a local winery and the moment Ava descended from the bus, recognition filled her eyes. She looked up at Max and gasped. "No way."

He grinned. "I know. I didn't believe it either. Who knew

THE COOKIE MATCH

these guys still had concerts on the weekend?" This was the pièce de résistance for their evening.

This time she grabbed his hand and they hurried along the sidewalk until they got to a path that would lead them over the grassy hill. Already country music filtered to them, along with cheers. The way her fingers laced with his made him feel like he could do anything. It was strange and exhilarating and he didn't want her to let go.

When they reached the top, she dropped his hand and stared out at the moderate crowd that had gathered in front of a stage. A band played while a young woman in jeans, a T-shirt, and a cowboy hat sang a familiar song.

Ava glanced over toward him and her eyes locked with his. "I can't believe it," she murmured. "How many of these did we sneak away to when we were in high school?"

"I lost count," he chuckled.

She let out a laugh and skittered down the hill toward the people below. He watched her go, reveling in the joy she showed. He'd been responsible for that joy. Max followed in her wake, finally catching up to her when she reached the edge of the crowd. She stood there, watching the musicians, the grin on her face spread wider than he'd ever seen.

The sun wouldn't be setting for another two hours. They had the rest of the evening to reconnect. He reached forward and tapped her shoulder, causing her to glance back at him. He nodded toward a blanket he'd brought when everyone was setting up and her eyes lit up.

"You just keep surprising me, you know that?" She moved past him and settled onto the blanket. They were far enough away from the stage that they didn't have to compete too much with the volume of the music.

Ava leaned back on her palms and lifted her face to the sky. The golden light reflected off her perfect skin and highlighted her hair. It was simple pleasures like this that spoke to her.

Somehow he knew that if he'd spent money on her—taken her to fancy restaurants or bought her lavish gifts, she would have turned her nose up at it. That was just who she was.

She must have felt his stare, because her eyes fluttered open and she turned her head so her chin rested on her shoulder. She shook her head and sat up straight. "Okay, so you've got my attention. We've walked down memory lane. And you're telling me that all you're trying to do is convince me that you haven't changed."

"Is that so hard to believe?"

"Yes, actually." She looked away, her lips pressed together tightly. "Sorry. I ..." Ava shook her head, clasping her hands together. "I shouldn't have generalized things so much earlier today. You're obviously not like those people we were always jealous of as kids. The ones who were so rich they could eat off gold plates and when I say jealous, I really mean we hated them for flaunting what we'd never have. Except, you became the same."

He watched her, understanding flooding his mind along with a slew of memories. They'd hated people who had a lot of money, but back then he'd thought it had been due to their lack of it. Now that he had plenty of flexibility when it came to his finances, he could say they'd been wrong.

Max nodded toward the book. "It's like that book, you know? There are bigger problems than social advancement and wealth. Relationships. Loyalty to the people you care about. That's what matters." His brow creased and he reached for a tuft of grass and rubbed it between his finger and thumb. Was it possible that by not keeping in touch with Ava he hadn't shown her the loyalty she deserved?

Ava's hand touched his and he met her gaze.

"It's kinda ironic." There was no question in his voice. "We sat around judging the people who had more than we did and that's exactly who I ended up becoming. I wasn't the friend I should have been and I regret that, Ava."

She flushed, withdrawing her hand again to brush aside some hair that had fallen in front of her face. When her eyes lifted to meet his, she let out a soft, almost nervous laugh. "I'm glad we can start over."

"Me too."

She reached for the book and flipped it open to the front page. *"My father's name being..."*

Max allowed himself to get lost.

Lost in her voice.

Lost in the words she spoke.

Lost in the story itself.

It had been so long since he'd felt this way while in the company of a woman, and he craved more. He lowered himself onto one elbow and watched her as she read to him. This was the kind of life he'd seen for himself, when he'd been younger.

And he hadn't really changed.

He might have come into wealth and fame, but he was still the same old Max he'd been years ago.

On the way home, darkness had fallen. They rode the bus all the way back to her grandmother's home and at some point she rested her head against his shoulder, only to end up falling asleep.

He smiled to himself as he placed his cheek against the top of her head. Maybe it wasn't such a crazy idea. Perhaps today was the first step they could take in the same direction. He didn't know a lick about the future, but he did know one thing.

Max wouldn't allow himself to lose Ava again.

Chapter Fourteen

Ava couldn't stop smiling.

So much so that several customers commented on it. It wasn't like she was exactly a grump most of the time. In fact, she'd prided herself on being a bubbly, outgoing barista who lifted the spirits of everyone who walked through the doors of Just Peachy.

Something must have been different about her smile today.

She refused to admit it had something to do with a certain someone. But each time she thought back to the night before, she simply couldn't fight the delight she felt.

On the way home she'd told him she'd figured out the menu and would be experimenting with her recipes tonight and he'd practically invited himself over.

Those giddy butterflies burst into flight within her and it was all she could do to keep her hands steady as she set to work making drinks. Max was going to stop by to see her.

And she couldn't wait.

"Someone met someone special last night," Trina sang as

she backed out of the supply room, a bag of cups in one hand and a sleeve of lids in the other."

"Actually, no. This time you're wrong," Ava countered. "I hung out with Max last night and he's coming by to try some recipes later."

By the look on Trina's face, Ava might have assumed that she'd said she planned on dressing up as a superhero and changing her career to billionaire vigilante. Trina's eyes bugged out and her mouth fell open. "Tell me you're joking."

"What?" Ava laughed. "You know he was a childhood friend."

"Yeah," Trina drawled, "but whenever you talked about him before, you never looked this happy."

Ava tossed a dirty rag at her friend, forcing a laugh as if that would save her from the conversation she knew was about to happen. "He's just a friend. I'm still swearing off guys. It was just refreshing to hang out with someone and not feel like all they wanted was more, more, more."

Trina slapped the cups onto the counter then placed a hand on her hip. "Are you sure that's not exactly what he's doing? We've both read the tabloids, Ava. The only time he's with a woman, it's for a show or a gala and then you never see them again."

"Which is why I fully intend on keeping everything *friendly* between us." Ava took the lids from her friend's hand and headed for the dispenser. "I promise. If anything more starts to develop, you'll be the first to know."

"I better be."

Ava pressed her lips together, but still the smile broke through. She might as well admit it to herself, if to no one else. Spending time with Max was refreshing. It was fun and carefree, just like it had been when they were kids. And he knew she didn't want anything more. So it would continue to be that way.

But what if you change your mind?

A quiet little voice in the back of her head dug up a very real question. What if she did change her mind? Was she getting too close to him? When he'd gone out of his way to make her remember their past, it had felt so good.

Was this what she'd been missing in a healthy relationship?

She shook off that thought before it could take root. There was a reason she had sworn off men. She needed to take time to *breathe*. It didn't matter how charming Max could be. It definitely didn't matter that they had a past. And it wouldn't matter if she started crushing on him again.

Ava had put her foot down and she wasn't going to let him sweep her off her feet.

❋

Well, darn it.

Ava stared at Max over the haphazard bouquet that looked like he'd picked it himself off the side of the highway. She could already envision him hunched over grabbing the morning glories that were in the fistful of blooms he carried.

He tilted his head like an adorable puppy as he held them out to her. "I figured you couldn't get mad at me if I arranged the flowers myself."

Ava bit down on the inside of her cheek—hard—so she didn't give away just how much this little gesture meant to her. Her fingers wrapped around the stems and she gazed down at them, her eyes burning with moisture.

"How could you?" she muttered.

"I'm sorry?"

She shoved the flowers back into his chest and spun on her heel to head toward the kitchen. His own shoes clipped along the floor, echoing through the quiet house until they came to a stop in the kitchen doorway.

Ava gripped the edge of the countertop, her head hanging low. All day she'd told herself she was perfectly content to keep things exactly as they were, but Trina's words must have invaded her thoughts and made her wonder if she was wrong.

"You don't have to keep them if you don't want ..." His voice drifted toward her, a heavy reminder that he was just as genuine and sweet as she had remembered.

She squeezed her eyes shut and shook her head. "They're perfect."

Silence hung in the air, weighing on her, crushing her spirit. Up until the moment when she'd opened that door, she'd known where she stood. She'd had a plan. She'd made rules.

"Ava? What's the matter?" This time his voice was so close that had she spun around too quickly, she likely would have collided with him. This was further confirmed when he touched her arm with his fingertips.

She jumped, then wiped her face on her shoulder before whirling around to face him. Max jumped back, but only a few inches. She scowled at him, then poked his chest for good measure. "You're what's wrong."

His nervous, crooked grin was so opposite of what he presented to the outside world. "I'm sorry? Is it something I did? I thought—"

"Of course it's something you did. You're *perfect*. Absolutely, freaking perfect."

He blinked a few times, his brows drawing together. "I'm sorry, I'm not following you. What exactly am I apologizing for?"

She threw her hands into the air, fully aware that she was acting irrationally. "I was having the perfect day, you know that? Last night was the perfect night."

"You keep saying that word like it's a bad thing," he mumbled.

Ava let out a laugh that sounded purely chaotic. "Yeah, maybe it is." She hugged herself, then leaned against the counter and looked at her feet. Taking in a few deep breaths, she attempted to calm her racing heart. She couldn't bring herself to look at him. The blush that quickly spread across her face was only one of the reasons. "Why did you have to go and ruin everything?" she whispered. "Why did you have to go and dredge up feelings I had for you?"

It was as if everything in the room had been put on pause. She could have heard the flap of a butterfly's wings if it weren't for the thundering of her own heart—which she was certain he could hear clear as day.

"Ava?"

Her head snapped up and her expression softened. Her heart felt trapped in her chest, demanding to be released. "I told you I wanted to swear off men. I needed to have some time to myself—to sort out some things."

"Yeah, I know."

"Well, you aren't making it very easy."

Finally there was a reaction behind his guarded expression. His eyes flickered with something almost carnal, a something that set her pulse on fire. He let out an exasperated breath. "Okay, I've tried to be patient, but you're talking in riddles and calling me names. I *really* feel like you think I did something wrong and yet you won't tell me. What's going on, Ava? Are you mad at me?"

This wasn't going anywhere. She couldn't find the words to tell him even if she tried. How was she supposed to explain to him that his little stunt the night before might have very well triggered deep feelings for him? His intentions hadn't been romantic. And yet here she was, swooning for him.

Ava closed her eyes briefly then threw her hands down to her sides. "Sorry. I'm just going through something." When she opened her eyes, he was still studying her. She inched away from him, forcing a smile. "Not to be that person, but maybe it's just ... you know ... life." She turned away from him, grimacing at the thought of blaming her outburst on something so ridiculous.

She yanked oven mitts from the counter and pulled them on one at a time. The oven timer beeped, saving her from having to pretend to check on the cookies and just pull them out. Ava grabbed the cookie sheet with one hand and waved her other hand over the top to fan the treats. Her smile was as fake as they came, but Max wouldn't be able to tell.

Placing the tray on the counter with a flourish, she gestured toward them. "Now you just have to wait for them to cool before I add the garnishes. You were a little early, you know."

Ava turned toward the fridge, but Max cut her off.

His arms were crossed over his chest and his expression had hardened to stone, the flowers forgotten near the edge of the counter where he'd been standing. "No."

She took a sudden step backward on instinct. He was far too close for the feelings that were still at the surface. Pushing aside those thoughts, she lifted a brow. "No? No what? You don't want me to put on the finishing touches? I really think I should—" She attempted to move around him but he blocked her again.

"No, you're not just going to brush off this argument and pretend it didn't happen. There's something bothering you. I can tell."

She let out a nervous laugh. "Nothing's bothering me. I'm just ... tired."

He worked his jaw back and forth, breathing heavily through his nose. She could almost imagine he'd turned into a dragon and was about to spew fire all over this kitchen. "Ava," he warned. "I brought you flowers and you got weird. That's not a normal reaction."

True.

"I didn't even spend a dime on them. Heck, I could get arrested for picking them. I have no idea if where I got them was private property.

Max stepped toward her and it took every ounce of strength not to edge away from him. She prayed he wouldn't touch her, because if he did, she knew she was a goner. One second of his skin grazing hers and the floodgates would be opened. "Ava," he whispered her name like it was sacred and goose bumps lifted on her arms. "What did I do that was so offensive to you?"

She tried scowling, really she did. She wanted to put up a thousand-foot wall between them—to ensure their friendship would remain unbroken—but at this point she'd already shattered it. Ava closed her eyes, digging deep for the strength to just tell him everything, and still she couldn't muster it.

He grasped her chin with his finger and thumb and her eyes flew open. There he was, begging her to just confess all.

Well, either he was going to regret it, or she would. Either way, someone wasn't going to be thrilled with what she was about to say.

Ava swallowed hard then steeled herself for his reaction. "I think I've fallen for you."

Chapter Fifteen

That was the very last thing Max would have expected to hear from Ava in this moment. The uphill battle he'd prepared himself for suddenly plateaued and he found himself at the top of the mountain overlooking the valley below.

All he could do was stare at her, unsure of how to express his utter joy at her words. He couldn't exactly confess that he'd hoped to do just that—to make her fall for him.

Ava tore away from him, backing up and rounding the island. "I knew you wouldn't be happy. I'm angry, too," she muttered with derision.

All at once he felt her slipping through his fingers.

No, he couldn't let this happen. He couldn't allow her to think he wasn't already on the same page. Max charged after her as she continued to pace and ramble.

"I told you I wasn't ready for another relationship. I *told* you that I needed a break and we were only supposed to be friends. And you *agreed*!" She threw her hands in the air with a sharp laugh. "You *promised* we'd be good. And then you had to go and mess everything up."

Max made it to her side. "Ava, you need to stop."

"You wanna know the worst part? This morning I still thought I was in control. I thought I'd found my best friend again and we could rewind time. I just didn't realize that I was a complete idiot."

"Ava," he commanded this time, but she still refused to listen. His hands shot out and he grasped her upper arms, giving her a gentle shake. "Ava! For Pete's sake! Will you shoosh?"

She snapped her mouth shut and her eyes grew wide.

"Good. Now listen to me, and listen well."

Ava opened her mouth but he shot her a fiery look that seemed to be enough to give her pause.

"I'm not going to apologize for any of it. Not pushing you to be the best version of yourself. Not rekindling our friendship. And certainly not making you fall in love with me."

Her only reaction was a few more blinks.

Max let his gaze sweep over her, and that rolling desire flared to life. "Do you have any idea how painful it was to have you so close and not be able to pull you into my arms? Last night nearly destroyed me, Ava. I got ready to come here tonight, not knowing if I would have the strength to be here and not confess that my feelings for you only continue to grow stronger. There is no smothering them, or stomping them out."

Ava's body seemed to lose some of its stiffness as she took in what he was saying. He released her arms, hoping he wouldn't regret doing so. Instead, he grasped her chin again so she wouldn't be tempted to look away.

"I couldn't sleep last night. I couldn't eat today. All I could think about was you and how I was supposed to live seeing you each day without calling you mine." His eyes searched hers for any indication this was what she wanted. There was still a very real possibility she was fighting her feelings for him and his confession was causing more damage than good.

Before he could utter another word, she put an end to his concerns. Ava clasped his face between both of her hands and pulled his lips hard against hers in a demanding, almost bruising kiss. Their bodies collided and he was bumped up against the island. The heat that had been a moderate flicker in his gut exploded with a vengeance, fully awake and demanding to be satiated.

Kissing Ava was like nothing he'd ever experienced before. Her passion, her drive, her zest for life all fed through her touch. His whole body hummed with an electrical current that could power the whole city, and all from one kiss.

She pushed her hands into his hair, weaving them through his waves as she clung to him like he was life itself.

Max pulled her tighter against himself, drinking in her soft form. If he were to die in this very moment, he wouldn't have a single regret. He'd gone to heaven in her embrace and wanted nothing more.

Their kiss deepened, dragging him farther and farther under an ocean's current that he thought might drown him if he wasn't pulled out. And just when he didn't think he'd be able to last a single second longer, Ava broke their kiss. She buried her face in his neck, their heavy breathing the only sound the kitchen had to offer.

Still she held onto him, clinging to him so he couldn't move. The haze that surrounded them both wouldn't be lifted any time soon. He lost track of time as they stood there and when she finally shifted in his arms, he relaxed his grip.

Ava glanced at him shyly, then scooted a few inches away. That was probably the smartest thing she'd done since he'd arrived. Their passion was as dangerous as unsupervised fireworks. One wrong move and the whole place would go up in flames.

She touched her lips with her fingertips, then turned away from him before leaning against the island.

Max didn't dare move. His dreams had come true. They were finally at a place where he could say there was a chance. And at the same time it felt like they were dangling from a thread over shark-infested waters.

He knew better than to believe he could just let her stand there and not hash it out. He hadn't gotten to where he was today without taking control and making things happen. "Ava," he murmured firmly, "we have to talk about this."

"I know," she said quietly. "Just let me think."

"You've been thinking for a few minutes already. It doesn't matter how long you stand there, I'm not going anywhere until you talk to me."

She turned around to face him, making sure to keep the island between them. Her hands grabbed onto the edge of the countertop and her eyes drilled into him. "What now?"

"What ... now? What now is that I'm not going to let you talk me out of this. I'm not going to let you tell me that we can't be something, because I know you felt it—that connection we had."

"But what if it's a fluke? What if you're just under a lot of stress with this charity thing, and I'm dealing with trying to get my catering business going. What if—"

"What if, nothing. Ava, you can't tell me that just a few minutes ago you didn't leave this existence and experience something amazing. That chemistry? I know I've never felt it with anyone before."

Her eyes dipped to the countertop and it appeared she attempted to hide her smile.

"See? You said so yourself. You're falling for me."

"Don't go getting a big head." Her gaze flitted up to meet his. "And I'm still not convinced this is a good idea, seeing as we're working together. We should probably really slow this down."

"Over my dead body."

Ava laughed and the sound was musical. That laugh alone was enough to make him believe that anything was possible. Slowly, he made his way toward her. "I don't care what it takes. We're going to figure this thing out. You and me. It's gonna happen." With each second that ticked by, he closed the distance between them. "I don't think it was a coincidence that we entered each other's lives when we did."

"You're right. It was Quinne, right? That's who you said tried to set us up? Or those matchmakers at the retirement community?"

He rolled his eyes and released an exaggerated groan. "It doesn't matter how it happened. All that matters is *this*." He took her chin in his grasp once more, and this time brushed his lips against her so lightly they could have been butterfly wings.

She closed her eyes. A whisper of a moan escaped her lips, and her hands came up to grasp him around the back of his neck.

Max pulled back just enough to get a good look at her when she opened her eyes. "See? This right here isn't something you come across more than once in your lifetime. This is special. And there's no way you're taking it from me."

The smile tugging at her lips won. She tilted her head to the side and her eyes seemed to dance. "Okay, so this is a thing. We're a thing."

"We're a thing," he repeated.

"It's about time."

Ava jumped, as did Max. They both whirled toward the intrusion, finding Rosalie standing in the doorway of the kitchen.

"Nana!" Ava laughed. "How long have you been there?"

"Long enough to think you two could star in my favorite romance soap opera."

Max laughed and Ava hid her face in his collar.

"I'm going to bed," Rosalie announced. "Make sure to lock up when you're done."

He waited until they could no longer hear her footsteps on the stairs before he glanced down at Ava. Her face was about as red as a cherry, but it only made her more beautiful in his eyes. "So ..." he whispered.

"So ..." she whispered back.

"You gonna make me some cookies?"

Ava pulled back and whacked his arm with the back of her hand. "Is that all you think about? Cookies?"

He shrugged, another chuckle forming on his lips. "Would you judge me if I admitted that I do it for the cookies?" Max snapped his fingers. "That could be the name of your bakery." He waved a hand across the air in front of him. "*Do it for the Cookies.*"

She snickered. "That's a terrible name."

"No, it's not. It's great. Then everyone will know that your cookie recipe is the best one there is. And everyone will come far and wide just to get a taste."

Ava placed a hand on her hip. "If I didn't know any better, I'd say you were drunk."

"Drunk on your love."

She shook her head with a laugh, then threw a rag at him. He ducked and it missed him by about three inches, landing behind him.

"Fine, we don't have to name it that. But after this charity event, you're going to have to come up with something, because there won't be a single person who won't know the name Ava Brooks and they're all going to want to know where to go to get their sugar fix."

She stopped what she was doing and stared at him. Her

brows creased, and the lines around her mouth deepened as she pressed her lips together.

"What's the matter?"

"Why are you so ... supportive?"

"That's a silly question."

Ava shook her head. "Not really. We've only just reconnected. But even before that kiss—"

"You mean that *amazing* kiss."

She gave him a flat look and he sobered. "As I was saying, even before we kissed, you were pushing me to do this—to follow my dreams."

"Why wouldn't I?"

"I don't know," she sighed. "Because our lives turned out so different from each other?"

"This isn't about the money again, is it?" He couldn't keep the exasperation out of his voice. "I told you. Money has nothing to do with it. We were cut from the same cloth. We grew up with the same kind of struggles. Just because I ended up where I am doesn't mean that those traits aren't still there."

"Yeah, you're right." She shook her head as if doing so would be enough to clear it. "You're totally right. I don't know what I was thinking."

His voice softened and he moved to stand behind her. Bringing his arms around her waist, he rested his chin on her shoulder. "You were thinking that you want us to be compatible."

She turned her face toward him slightly but not so much he could see both of her eyes. "That makes sense."

"Of course it does. Because you're smart and you think ahead. You're the kind of person who likes to have fun, but you also know when you need to buckle down and prepare. Those are the kinds of traits I love about you."

Ava leaned into him. "I can't believe it."

"You can't believe what?" He murmured, trailing kisses along her neck.

Her breath hitched in her chest. "I can't believe we never let this happen when we were in high school. Can you imagine what our life would have been like if we had decided to date?"

Somehow he knew exactly where they'd be. He probably would have asked her to marry him a long time ago.

That realization hit him harder than he would have expected and the air felt like it had been knocked from his body.

"Max?"

He grunted.

"You okay?"

"I'm perfect," he smiled.

Chapter Sixteen

Over the next couple of days, Ava buried herself in her recipes. She needed them to be perfect. Everything from the amount of sugar she sprinkled over her shortbread cookies to the amount of lemon in her meringue filling had to be exact. All of the cookies needed to be uniform, as if they'd come off a factory line.

All of this work didn't afford much time for her to see Max, but that was okay. He was busy with his own stuff and they managed to find time to see each other—mostly to hide away in coat closets to make out.

The passion they shared was so much stronger than she would have ever expected. She only had to be with him for five minutes and she felt as though her body had been set on fire and she wasn't able to move her legs without fearing she'd lose her balance and end up as a puddle on the floor.

Yes, it was smarter to take Max in smaller doses, rather than get burned out all at once.

Then there was work.

The more time she spent on her recipes, the harder it was getting to make herself head to her job. The customers at *Just*

Peachy were still great. The change had happened in herself. She'd started to notice just how grumpy they could be in the morning. Their attitudes wore on her more and more each shift and she found herself wishing she could just escape out the back and get to work on the next new creation.

Rather than fixate on those issues, she found herself fantasizing about Max. Her life had only continued to improve. She couldn't think of a single reason why she would want anything to change.

So, when she headed up the elevator to Max's floor at the end of the workday, she was surprised to find him pacing angrily in his office.

"I don't care what you say, Mother. You know what you did, and you don't even care."

She paused right outside the door, waiting for him to get off the phone. His secretary glanced in her direction a few times, her expression indifferent.

"No, you can't just expect me to give in and tell you it's okay." He stopped pacing in front of his window, one hand behind his back clenching and unclenching. "Yes, I know it's been years. But are you ever going to stop trying to control everything? I'm hanging up now." He ended the call and tossed the phone on his desk, only then noticing Ava standing there.

His expression immediately shifted from anger to one of warmth and welcome.

"Ava. I wasn't expecting you."

She lifted two cups of coffee—now a tradition. "I thought you could use some coffee. Decaf." He moved toward her, taking the cups in his hands and brushing a kiss on her cheek. "Now that you're here, maybe we could get some dinner."

"That sounds nice." His prior conversation stuck in her head and she watched him walk across the room to place the coffees on the desk. "Will your mother be joining us?"

Max stiffened, his hands still wrapped around the cups. Though he didn't face her, she knew he'd been taken off guard and not in a good way.

Ever since they'd first caught up, she'd thought there was too much contention between Max and his mother. She hadn't known the best way to bring it up, and the idea continued to fester in the back of her mind. Listening to the way he'd spoken to Lily tore at her heart. Whatever mistakes Max's mother had made were clearly still a big issue for him, but that didn't mean she shouldn't be forgiven. Ten years was a long time to hold on to that much anger.

He finally turned to face her after several seconds of silence. "No. My mother won't be joining us."

"Will we be spending any time with her together?"

"What is this fascination you have with my mother? Did she contact you? Because if she did—"

"No, of course not. I just thought it would be nice to get to know her better, just like we are."

His eyes narrowed. The judgment was so clearly pooling in his gaze that she had to force herself not to react. This was one of those moments when she would probably be better off minding her own business.

Ava forced a smile. "Never mind, forget I said anything. I wasn't thinking."

Still, Max studied her. She looked away, but it did nothing to ease the tension she'd brought into the room. *Change the subject.* That's what she needed to do. Ava moistened her lips and glanced at him once more. "Where do you want to go to dinner?"

There was a split second when she thought Max wouldn't go for the shift in topic. But then he smiled. His arms crossed over his chest and he tilted his head slightly. "How about someplace special?"

"Special?" she said it with caution. "Max, you know I don't like—"

"I know. You don't like it when I spend a lot of money on you. But I have business or social obligations I can't change and it would mean the world if you would be at my side, at least sometimes. You and me against the world again."

There was a small girl inside her who had always dreamed of being whisked away by a charming prince and rescued from the dreary life she'd led all these years.

Max was that prince. And this was her moment.

There was only one problem.

"This is going to sound lame but I don't have anything to wear that is nice enough for a special place."

He grinned. "Now that's a problem I can help solve."

There was no time to argue with him. Max swiftly moved across the room toward the door. "Cathy, get that boutique on the phone. The one where I get my suits tailored. Tell them I'm bringing a special guest and we need to find a dress for this evening." He turned to face her, glee written all over his face. "There. Problem solved."

❋

Ava dragged her clammy hands down the silk dress in an attempt to dry them off, but it didn't help. She fidgeted in the entryway of the hotel that housed one of the fanciest restaurants in the city. When Max had said *something nice*, she hadn't expected *this nice*.

This place had it all.

A chandelier.

Marble statues.

And ceilings that rose higher than some of the buildings on this block.

Max stood to the side speaking with someone dressed far

too nicely to be the hostess, and this time she knew she was right because the hostess was speaking to another couple and was about to walk off and seat them at their table.

Ava's whole body seemed to hum with the anticipation of being on a real date with *the* Maximus Stone. She had expected to be swarmed by the paparazzi by now, but so far they'd been able to keep it really low-key.

Again she rubbed her hands on her dress, only to have one of them snatched away and slipped into Max's.

Her head whipped around to find Max standing beside her. He brought her hand to his lips with a smile. "Don't be nervous. It's just dinner."

"Yeah," she muttered under her breath, "at a restaurant where the meals probably cost more than my monthly phone plan."

He chuckled, but the warm honey sound did nothing to put her at ease.

"I told you, Max, this place isn't for me. I wasn't—we weren't raised to be comfortable in places like this."

Max gave her a firm look. "No more of that. Did it take a while for me to get used to the money I got from my father? Sure. But it didn't change who I am. And spending it on you now and then doesn't make either of us lesser people."

She blew out a frustrated sigh. "Yeah, I know." He'd never understand why she felt so out of place. Maybe he would have a long time ago, but they were very different people.

What if they were too different?

That wasn't fair to say. Max had already proven that he was the kind of man she could see herself with. That night at the winery. Their evenings as she worked on her recipes. Maximus was still plain old Max, who she'd grown to care for when she was younger.

Ava could swallow her nerves for one night and be the woman Max needed her to be. One night. That's all this was.

Then they could discuss parameters for the future. It wasn't like he was expecting her to become a housewife who only hung on his arm at events.

Unless he was ...

Those thoughts would lead her down a dangerous road if she wasn't careful. Time to live in the moment and see what being on the other side of the glass was all about.

Max squeezed her hand, then gestured for her to follow the man in the tux. Ava leaned into him, basking in the warmth and joy she felt when she was around him. If there was one thing about Max she had missed it was his ability to make her feel safe and wanted. She'd never had to worry that he didn't accept her for exactly who she was.

She craned her neck around and gazed up at the man she had so easily fallen in love with. He grinned down at her and in that moment she could see her happily ever after. There were no worries about money or the future. They were together and that was all that mattered.

"Here you are, Mr. Stone. The table you requested."

Ava shot Max a surprised look. "You ask for a specific table, huh? *Fancy*."

He waved a dismissive hand. "Only because this is the place with the best view."

"The best view ..." That was when she had a chance to really look off toward where Max motioned and get a good look at a fountain bathed in color. Water shot up into the air as if it had studied with the best ballerinas in the world. It floated and pranced, changing colors as it did. Ava's eyes widened as she settled into her seat, mesmerized. "I can't believe I didn't notice this as we came in."

To be fair, she was a little too mesmerized by a certain someone to really pay attention to the aesthetics of the rest of the restaurant.

Soft instrumental music played, complementing the water

that splashed back into the fountain. A low hum of voices from neighboring tables completed the ambience of the place and she understood now more than ever what she'd been missing out on when she didn't have the money to go to places like this.

She'd missed out on beauty, on atmosphere, on experiences she could only dream of.

On the one hand, she couldn't contain the excitement that came with having Max in her life—to have someone who wanted to share this side of the world with her. But on the other, she found it hard not to get sick to her stomach.

Ava placed a hand on her stomach and she must have grimaced because Max leaned forward with concern. "Are you okay?"

She nodded. "Just a little like a fish out of water."

He glanced around the restaurant. "Do we need to go? We can get something and take it home with us."

Shaking her head, she reached across the table and took his hand in her own. "Of course not. We're here, and I'm determined to enjoy myself." She forced a smile. Hopefully, these kinds of sensations wouldn't last long. If she wanted to see how far this relationship with Max could go, she needed to find a way to fit in.

Chapter Seventeen

Admittedly, Max knew he should have started out small. He should have taken Ava somewhere she could ease into the lifestyle he'd come to take for granted. As soon as he saw the blood drain from her face, he'd regretted the decision to bring her to his favorite restaurant.

But from the looks of it, Ava was going to be fine. It was a rough start, but then she'd smiled and said she wanted to enjoy the evening. He watched her as she looked over her menu, and he no longer felt the need to tell her that he would make it up to her.

She smiled over the edge of the leather binding and he smiled back. He could have taken out a hundred women but he'd never feel like he did in this moment.

Being here with Ava just felt *right*.

If only he hadn't missed all of those years with her and there was only one person to blame.

Max shoved the thought aside and glanced over his own menu. Everything might not be perfect yet, but it would be. They were capable of figuring it out.

Ava moaned, and Max chuckled at the look of utter ecstasy on her face. "It's that good, huh?"

She rolled her eyes back. "You tasted it. Have you ever had tiramisu as good as this?"

He leaned forward with his fork extended and she yanked the dish toward her, shaking her head.

"You only get one bite. That was the deal."

Max glanced down at his own chocolate mousse. "Well, this is just as good."

Ava shook her head again with a laugh. "Don't kid yourself. This is amazing." Her eyes shot wide and she gasped. He jumped, glancing around, expecting her to point out something scandalous, but he didn't see anything. "I should make a version of this as a cookie! It could be a macaron with tiramisu filling." She held out her hand and snapped her fingers. "I need a pen."

He gave her a dumbfounded look. "And you think I have one?"

"You have pockets, don't you?"

"Well, yeah, but—"

She made a show of gesturing to her own dress. "Does it look like I can fit a pen anywhere on my person?"

His eyes swept over her form and his gut tightened. Now was not the time to be thinking of her that way. He chewed on the inside of his cheek, fighting back his smile. "No, I don't suppose you could."

"I need a pen," she repeated.

Max shook his head. "For someone who keeps insisting she comes from nothing, you sure know how to make demands."

She gasped with feigned offense, but before she had a chance to make a snarky comment, he waved over one of the nearby servers.

The young woman came across. "Is there anything I can get for you?"

He motioned toward her little black apron. "You don't happen to have a pen we could borrow in that pocket of yours, do you?"

"And a piece of paper?" Ava asked hopefully.

He chuckled again. "And a piece of paper."

The waitress smiled warmly. "Of course." In a matter of seconds she'd retrieved a pad of paper and a pen. She tore off the top sheet with a flourish and held it out to him. "Is there anything else I can get for you?"

"No, I think that about does it."

Her smile widened before she headed off.

"Oooh. I think someone likes you," Ava teased, snatching the paper and pen from his hand.

"What? Because of her smile? She's just being friendly."

"Yeah," Ava drawled. "Because I throw huge smiles at every handsome young man who comes to the coffee shop."

He stiffened. "You do?"

"No," she laughed, then she scribbled something on the paper in front of her. When she peeked at him he was caught still staring at her. "Why? Would that make you jealous?"

Max gazed at her, already knowing the answer to that question. It was a simple one, something he wasn't necessarily proud of. When he didn't respond right away, her hands stilled. Slowly she glanced up at him.

His voice was as serious as it could get when he finally spoke. "Yes, I think it would."

Her smile faded and not for the first time he regretted something he'd said to her. But he was being honest; that was what she needed from him.

"I love you, Ava."

The room went silent, or at least that was how it felt. All he could hear was the sound of his own heart. All he could feel

THE COOKIE MATCH

was the thundering in his chest. He hadn't meant to confess his love so soon, and definitely not in a place where she didn't feel comfortable. He'd wanted to say it on level terms.

Right now, the only thing he could think about was the fact that she hadn't said it back. But why would she? This was all still too new. She hadn't even wanted a relationship in the first place.

Max cleared his throat and looked away. He wasn't about to make her say anything. That would be worse than springing those words on her. Rather than make a big deal about this, he grabbed his spoon and took another bite of his chocolate mousse.

After his heart had settled down he glanced over toward Ava, noting that she'd become hyper focused writing her notes. When she was done, she folded up the paper and held it tightly in her hand.

He'd long since paid for their food and the longer they stayed, the more awkward it became. "Let's head home, yeah?"

Ava pressed her lips together, then nodded. "Yeah."

Still no comment. No proclamation of love. No indication that she'd even heard what he'd said. Well, two could play at that game. He didn't have to say a single word. They could pretend.

And that's what they did.

They pretended all the way to the car.

They pretended on the drive back to her place.

And they pretended as he walked her to her front door.

Ava seemed to need to fill the void of conversation with information on how she'd pull off the recipe for her cookies. Most of it was gibberish to him and while he would have loved nothing more than to hear her say those three special words to him, he couldn't deny that he enjoyed listening to her talk.

They stopped at the door and Ava's rambling faded. She

gestured toward the door. "I suppose I should get inside before Nana comes out to see how things went."

"And how did things go?" He shouldn't have even asked the question. It was reaching and he knew it.

She smiled timidly.

"Ava," he whispered. "If I did something ... said something ... to offend you, I'm—"

"You didn't do anything wrong," she murmured. "I promise."

"Then why—"

Ava pressed her lips together, her gaze searching the ground before she finally lifted them up to meet his. "You know that I didn't want to jump into a relationship."

"Yeah."

"And I did."

He could already see where this was going. It couldn't be clearer. "I sense there's a *but* coming."

She placed a hand to his cheek. "There's a lot I don't know."

This was definitely the part where she told him they were taking things too fast. "It's okay, Ava. You don't have to—"

"The whole way here, I've been thinking about it."

"Really. I get it. I got carried away—"

"And I needed to know for certain this is what I want."

He took a step back, holding up a hand and preparing to head back to his car.

"I love you too, Max," she whispered.

Max went stock still. He glanced at her, unsure he'd heard her correctly.

Ava lifted her shoulders then dropped them listlessly. Her eyes brimmed with emotion. "I love you," she repeated. "But I'm scared. I'm *so* scared that—"

He scooped her up into his arms, crushing her against his body. Ava clung to him as if her life depended on him and

THE COOKIE MATCH

only him. Relief and pure joy exploded within him. If he were honest with himself, he'd admit that some part of his life depended on her, too.

Max pulled back just far enough to gain access to her face. He held it between both of his hands and pressed a hard, demanding kiss to her lips. When he released her, he tossed his head back and let out a whoop and a laugh.

Ava hugged herself, her laughter joining his. "I guess that's it then? There's no going back?"

"Definitely not," he murmured.

"So, what now?"

"What now? Are you seriously asking me to tell you what our future looks like?"

"You always used to talk about it."

"I know," he grinned. "I always had a plan, because I always needed to know what would happen next."

"And that's why I'm asking you." Her voice had returned to that timid sound. "I think I've gotten to the point where I don't want surprises."

Max's brows shot upward. "Really?" Ava was changing before his eyes and he couldn't say he was disappointed.

She flushed. "I'm getting too old to fly by the seat of my pants, Max. You've ruined me."

He threw back his head and laughed. "Do you hear yourself?"

"What?" Ava demanded. "I thought you would have been glad to hear that I don't want to just wing it."

"And I thought you were all about having fun. And what if I told you that I was perfectly happy to just spend time with you and see where things might go, take it one day at a time?" Yes, that was a stretch, in all reality, they needed to be able to find good middle ground.

She stared at him blankly.

He laughed again, pulling her in for another hug and

resting his chin on her head. "I'll make you a promise, though. How about we get through this event that you're helping to cater, and then we can talk about where you want your future to go. We can let this whole 'you and me' thing settle just a little before we decide what we want to do with it."

"I think I can agree to something like that."

"Have you given it any thought?"

"What? Us?"

He shook his head as she turned her face and rested her cheek against his chest. "No," he mumbled. "The idea your nana and I had about you making this catering thing more than just a one-time gig."

Ava pulled back and peered up at him. "You mean to make it permanent? Like a bakery or something?"

"That's exactly what I'm suggesting."

She gave him a crooked grin. "I would be lying if I said I hadn't thought that far ahead."

"So you have considered it."

"Well, I did ask to be paid enough to cover a down payment on a little place. And I think if this goes well, perhaps it's something that I'd enjoy doing."

He grinned. "I knew it."

"And while we're on the matter of difficult subjects, what about you?"

His smile faded. "What *about* me?"

"Your mother. You seem so distant from her. As if your relationship is broken."

Max's heart stopped. His gaze darkened and his voice lowered. "There is no relationship."

"Max," she said, "I don't like seeing how unhappy that makes you. You've convinced me to consider a career shift. I would like to convince you to consider making a change with your mother."

His jaw tightened. This moment between them had been

so good—something that he'd wanted since before he could remember. He didn't want to ruin it by getting in a fight over his mother. So he did the only thing that would make it go away. "Fine. I'll consider it."

Ava's smile of relief only mildly pleased him. At some point he'd explain what Lily had done to both of them and she'd agree that he was right.

That might not be tonight, but it didn't have to be. It'd happen soon enough. For now, he'd just be happy she was his.

Chapter Eighteen

Ava couldn't believe how much her life had changed since Max came back into it. Everything she'd wanted but never knew how to acquire had managed to fall right into her lap. Ava had never been one to believe in fate. That just wasn't her thing.

She liked to find her happiness wherever that might be, and perhaps that was why she'd chosen to steer clear of planning. If she didn't plan, she didn't have to be disappointed.

That was beginning to change. She could see herself in a future alongside Max, working at a bakery that she willingly poured her blood, sweat and tears into. They had a family, with lots of kids and they were happy.

Each time she allowed herself to fall into this daydream, she had to pull herself out of it because who really knew what was in the future?

Max and Ava had found themselves in a nice little routine. Whether they met up at Maple Gardens so she could use the kitchen Peter had offered, or they hung around her nana's place, they managed to find plenty of time to spend with one another.

THE COOKIE MATCH

Ava pulled a tray of cookies out of her nana's oven and placed it on the stovetop.

"That smells amazing," Max murmured from the other side of the kitchen. Seated at the table, surrounded by paperwork, his tie hanging askew, he looked like he'd just walked off Wall Street. Surprisingly, even looking like that, Ava found him irresistible. There was something about the way he carried himself that was so different from when they were younger and she couldn't get enough.

Ava waved her oven mitt through the air to dissipate the heat coming off the tray. "I think I've finally figured out these crème brûlée macarons I was telling you about," she called over her shoulder. "They came out absolutely perfect and now all I have to do is wait for them to cool before I put in the filling."

A pair of arms wrapped around her middle and she gasped. His chin rested on her shoulder and his soft voice sent a fresh shock wave of shivers down her spine. "I knew you could do it."

She rested her hands over his and leaned into him, a soft hum escaping her chest, much like the purr of a cat. "I don't think I could have done it without you."

"None of that crazy talk," he murmured again. "I firmly believe you would have ended up here in the end."

Ava grinned. "Maybe. But you and Nana were the ones who gave me the push I needed."

"I'll take all the credit and more." Max spun her around and pressed a lingering kiss to her lips.

The way he could make her feel, like she was floating from a simple touch, still filled her with awe. She couldn't recall feeling this euphoria with any other guy she'd dated. It was as if her soul innately knew that Max had always been meant for her.

That was silly right?

Their kiss deepened, the sparks and chills intensified. There was no way that they didn't have an otherworldly connection. Nothing else made sense. Ava had to be the first to pull away from their kiss due to her legs going completely numb. She exhaled breathily before settling a dazed look on him. "You probably shouldn't be doing that."

He chuckled, his focus shifting to her face as he brushed aside a stray hair. "Why not?"

"Because I can't guarantee that I won't collapse right here as I turn to jelly." She'd whispered it, unable to use her full voice. "I still can't believe this is happening. It feels like a fairy tale."

"And maybe it is." His eyes dipped to meet hers once more. "Who's to say that it's not."

A shy smile tugged at her lips. "Coming from a guy who always had a plan, your statement doesn't quite sound like you."

He scoffed. "Maybe I've evolved. Perhaps I've spent the last several years wishing I'd done more to get you back in my life. I'm capable of change, you know."

"Oh, I know." She slipped her arms around his neck and threaded her fingers through his hair. "Which is why I know eventually you're going to give in and talk to your mother—air this all out so you two can reconcile."

She realized her mistake the second his eyes clouded over, as they usually did when she brought up Lily.

Max pulled away. "I don't understand why you keep pressuring me to talk to her. Nothing can change what she's done. And I've made the decision not to have her toxicity in my life."

The warmth she'd felt being in his arms disappeared like steam rising in the air, despite the still-hot oven at her back. She'd told him before about how her mother's death had affected her and how she wished she still had her mother in her life. Family relationships were sometimes the only thing that people had when times got tough. He had to understand that.

But it just didn't seem to be clicking with him.

Ava kept her mouth clamped tight so she didn't make matters worse. They'd gone through this exact conversation once before since he'd told her he'd consider reconciling with his mother and it had turned out similarly. Max was just being stubborn. That was all.

He raked a hand through his hair, tugging on its ends then muttered, "I know I said I'd consider it, and I have."

She knew what was coming before he even uttered the words. And already her heart was breaking—for him and his mother alike.

"I'm not going to do it. She made her choices and I'm allowed to make mine."

"I never said you weren't," Ava said quietly, trying not to get defensive at the implication of his words. "I'm not forcing you to do anything."

Max's eyes widened. "You aren't? Because it sure seems like you are. Any time we have a quiet moment like this where I feel like we're getting closer, you bring her up. It's like she's this barrier that you have to keep between us. It's not like I've cut her completely out of my life. What's the problem with keeping things the way they are?"

Heat seared her cheeks. Max had asked that same question before. He was pushing back against her again and she was seeing it more and more recently. She had to press her lips together so tightly that they started to tingle before she said something she regretted. He wasn't in the right state of mind to discuss this. He was frustrated and getting himself wound up.

"No comment?" He let out a mirthless chuckle.

"That's not fair," she blurted. "You know that family is important to me, and—"

"Well, not to me," he cut in.

Her head reared back and she blinked a few times.

He seemed to realize what he'd said, because his whole countenance shifted. His features softened and his shoulders dropped. "You know that's not what I meant. You're important to me. And only you. I don't need my mother in my life to be fulfilled."

She shook her head. "That's not how it works, and you know it."

"Maybe I don't." He looked away and rubbed the back of his head before dropping his hand to his side. "Honestly? I just want you. I want us to start a family of our own and be able to make new traditions and new memories. Everything about my mother just leaves a sour taste in my mouth."

"It wouldn't if you'd only reconcile with her." This was her last-ditch effort. "You talk of us creating new memories so why wouldn't it work with your mom? You can't just love some parts of me and exclude my need for a happy family."

Max's jaw tightened. He shook his head, not uttering a single word, before he turned and gathered his paperwork.

"Max—"

"You know what? That's a pretty low blow. You stand there telling me that I should do something I don't want to, because it would prove I love you. How is that fair?"

"That's not what I meant."

"You know what it reminds me of? That time when Kev told you that you couldn't visit your childhood friend."

His statement was like a slap to the face. "That's different and you know it."

Once again, Max shook his head. "It's really not all that different. Both are ways people try to control others." He placed his paperwork in a folder. "I think I should go before we take this conversation to somewhere we'll regret."

"Yeah, maybe you should." She almost spat the words.

Max stared at her. She couldn't tell if he was surprised or if he was just angry. Their little staring contest lasted only until she had to tear her gaze from him. She faced her tray of cookies and muttered. "I'll see you later."

"Yeah, see you later," he returned.

She heard his footsteps cross the floor, then the front door opening and shutting far quieter than she would have managed had the situation been flipped. How could he accuse her of being controlling? She was the opposite of controlling.

Did she want him to fix his relationship with his mother? Of course she did. Lily wasn't toxic. She'd made a few mistakes in her life, but she shouldn't have to pay for them until her death. He had to see that.

She let out a heavy breath, hating how easy it was for them to be at odds with each other. Max had a right to be upset with Lily. But his anger was only festering the longer he kept it inside him.

Maybe it was simply too late for him to change. He'd harbored his fury for so long it had become its own entity. It was a demon within him that he would have to battle on his own if he ever had a hope of healing from it.

There was only one problem.

He had to first accept he had something he needed to heal before he'd make the changes necessary to make progress. And if there was one thing she knew about Max, it was that he didn't think anything was wrong with him or his relationship with his mother.

Chapter Nineteen

Max was on edge. Unsettled. There was no doubt about it. He'd slowly felt it creeping in on him from the moment Ava came into his life, and he'd chosen to ignore it. The simple fact was, the closer he got to Ava the more he resented his mother.

He didn't regret the state of his relationship with Lily one bit. In fact, the more he fell for Ava, the more he realized he'd been *too* easy on his mother over the past several years. She'd taken something from him that he'd never be able to get back.

If Lily hadn't ripped him from his school and taken him from the city where he'd grown up, he might have realized his attraction for Ava sooner and they might have been together for years—perhaps even have a family by now.

He was upset about the lost time, the what-ifs, and no one seemed to understand where he was coming from.

Ava was making him feel guilty and his mother was doing what she always did and trying to pretend nothing was wrong. All of it was giving him a big headache and it needed to stop.

Rather than heading home after leaving Ava's place, Max went to his office. His apartment felt too lonely when he was there by himself, ironic seeing as he'd never really shared it with anyone before. At least the quiet of the office was tolerable, with the presence of the security guards and the janitorial staff.

He spent the better part of the night fidgeting and pacing as he tried to come up with excuses as to why he shouldn't even feel guilty.

Because he didn't. Max had made his choices after his mother had made hers. He'd thought long and hard how he was going to treat his mother after what she did, and he wasn't going back.

A growl rumbled from his chest, crashing through the quiet of his empty office, but it did nothing to release the fury he currently experienced, feeling like Ava was no longer on his side. He should have expected she'd be persistent about trying to get him to reconcile with his mother. But every time she brought it up, they were having a nice moment. He was beginning to wonder if she was doing it on purpose.

Even his face ached from the perpetual scowl he wore. He could feel every crevice, every line in his forehead and between his brows. If he were a lesser man, he might have trashed his office, throwing and breaking things just to release his pent-up energy. Thankfully, with his upbringing, he'd come to value his belongings and understood that while he could now replace them, a tantrum wouldn't solve anything.

Max stopped in his place and took in a deep breath. Logically, he shouldn't even be upset with Ava. She was only trying to help.

He was perfectly happy to spend time with her family. She should be willing to keep his out of it.

Eventually, she'd get it. He just needed to remain firm in what he'd told her tonight.

Ava wasn't unreasonable. She was just the sunshine compared to his grumpiness.

Max kept his distance from Ava for a couple days. Unfortunately, one of those days was a scheduled visit with his mother—one he couldn't avoid.

Begrudgingly, he showed up at Maple Gardens and headed toward the common area where they usually had their visits. Most of his visits were on game days, and today was bingo. To be distracted during his visit helped him avoid excessive conversation where he would have to discuss his feelings and the way he still felt about his mother.

They sat across from each other as the next number was called.

"B-twelve."

Max stared hard at his card. If he even glanced up at his mother he knew he'd probably say something or do something he would regret. The last thing he needed was to make a scene where his mother lived and at the place where he had found a new caterer.

It would be far better to suffer in silence.

"N-thirty-seven."

His mother placed a marker on her card, then shifted in her seat. Once or twice she cleared her throat. But that was how most of these events went. But then, unexpectedly, she said his name. "Maximus?"

He clenched his jaw so tight it ached.

"Sweetheart? I can't help but feel that something is different about you."

As if against his will, his gaze darted up to meet hers. "You don't know anything about me. You haven't since I found out about my father."

She didn't react. Lily knew how to maintain her cool, something apparently he hadn't inherited from her. He clearly struggled with keeping his emotions in check.

"I can see that something is going on. I know you don't like discussing much with me, but I'm willing to listen if you want to talk."

His gaze hardened. "I'm not discussing anything with you. You know you lost that right a long time ago."

Lily nodded. "Yes, I know."

Max didn't know what came over him, but hearing her speak with that despondent tone ripped through him harder than he'd expected. The guilt and grief from his conversation with Ava returned with a vengeance and he heard her lecture in his head over and over again.

The anger returned, but mostly because he was angry at himself for being so weak he couldn't stand his ground. If there was one rock he was willing to die on, it was this one. He'd keep his relationship alive, but only just. His mother had raised him, kept a roof over his head—so that much she deserved.

"I'm not going to talk about anything with you, because frankly you're the problem."

Still no reaction. He'd said all of this before. The shock value had all but faded.

"I'm dating Ava now. You remember her?"

His mother nodded. "Yes."

"We bumped into each other and I realized a lot about the kind of person you were. Imagine my surprise when I found out she'd called when she moved in with her nana and left a new phone number for me. A phone number I somehow never received." He let out a quiet laugh and leaned forward, ready to drop a bomb on her he was sure would at least register some shock. "Get this. She thinks that you and I need to reconcile."

He wasn't disappointed. Though his mother didn't react as much as he'd wanted her to, her brows still lifted with disbelief.

"Don't get your hopes up. I told her that she was wrong. The relationship we have isn't going to change, at least not any time soon. There was already far too much baggage, even before I found out about Ava."

"Do you care for her?"

He stared at her, his own incredulity rising to the surface. "That's all you want to know? Do I care for her?" Max smacked his palm to his forehead. "I don't understand you."

"No, I don't suppose you would."

That caught his attention and he stared at his mother like she'd grown an extra set of eyes. She'd never said something like that to him before. Every conversation they'd had since she'd come to live at Maple Gardens had been one-sided.

Lily got to her feet and stared down her nose at him. The other residents around them stopped what they were doing to watch whatever was just about to unfold. She put the bingo markers from her hand on the table, took a deep breath, then released it. "I had reasons for my decisions, including the one about your father. They were wrong reasons and I wish I'd been less afraid of losing you... not that it mattered because I lost you anyway. I've tried to explain. You've refused to listen. People make mistakes. We all do, including you. Some are bigger than others—"

He huffed, glancing at those around him like they might be on his side, but no one seemed to disagree with his mother.

"At this point in time, while I still love you and want you in my life, I no longer wish to endure the kind of negativity you insist on bringing with you."

Max couldn't move. He'd been turned to stone from her stare and her words. Was she actually telling him she no longer wanted him to visit her? That didn't sound right. She'd been the one who insisted on him paying her monthly visits. She'd been the one who continued to request they talk about what

THE COOKIE MATCH

had happened. It was strange, this feeling that he was about to lose something he'd hadn't even wanted.

His mother gave him a hard look. "I officially release you from any obligation you feel to visit me."

He opened his mouth, unsure of what he was going to say at that moment. Part of him wanted to argue with her. What would everyone think? She couldn't just refuse to see him. Did he even want to continue seeing her? This could be exactly what he needed to finally move on—to do it without dwelling on everything he'd lost.

Lily stared at him expectantly, as did those who surrounded them. He was put on the spot. Somewhere in the back of his mind he realized that even the person who had been calling out the bingo numbers had stopped.

He swallowed down the unexpected ache and shame he felt in this moment, something that seemed to slap him clear across the face. Still, he couldn't bring himself to accept that she made a good point.

Max was still in the right. He was allowed to feel betrayed by his mother and he was allowed to cope any way he felt would help. It wasn't like he berated his mother at every turn. He still visited her when she requested. He simply refused to share his life with her in the way most sons shared their lives with their parents.

Slowly, he got to his feet. "Okay. If that's what you want, then that's what you'll get." He let his gaze sweep through the room, then shook his head. "Goodbye, Mother."

He thought when he walked out of the building he would feel a weight lifted from his shoulders. He even prepared for it the second his foot hit the pavement.

But nothing happened.

If anything, he felt even more at odds with himself. Something didn't quite feel right. Whether it was the way he'd left things, or the fact that she was the one who flipped the table on him, it didn't matter.

Max stopped and stared at the building, confusion flooding his mind. If Ava were here, she'd tell him she'd told him so. Hadn't she been telling him this whole time that he needed to heal the wounds between himself and his mother?

The ache inside his chest intensified. There was no way he was going to go back in there with his tail between his legs. Now they both got what they wanted—to be left alone.

He marched over to his car and got inside. There was one good thing that had come out of this—more time he could spend on what really mattered.

His job.

And Ava.

Chapter Twenty

Ava couldn't shake the feeling of unease after the argument she'd had with Max. They'd had their ups and downs since they'd become friends as kids. Even when they were in high school they'd have days when they didn't want to see each other.

Did this mean they were broken up?

No. She didn't get that feeling at all.

They were just going through a rough patch.

It didn't matter how many times she checked her phone. She knew he hadn't messaged or called, because he was still the same stubborn Max that she had befriended all those years ago.

Rather than dwell on what was going on with her love life, she focused on diving into work. She'd missed a few days at the coffee shop with all her extra time on the catering gig and it was nice to be back in her element.

Folks came and went, ordering their usual and leaving a little bit happier than they'd come in. She paid closer attention to the couples who came in, something she hadn't used to do. The way they would show their love for one another seemed to tug at her more than before. She found herself yearning to connect with Max again, even if it was only for him to tell her she was wrong.

Soon it was time for her to take a break and she grabbed a croissant from the display case before heading over to a table in the corner. Maybe she should call him, ask him if he was doing okay. If he didn't pick up, she'd know he needed more time.

Ava had picked up her phone when a shadow fell across her table. For the briefest of moments she thought Max had come to visit her at the coffee shop to apologize and her heart had ripped right out of her ribcage.

Except it wasn't Max.

"Kev?"

"Hi, Ava."

Her whole body tensed. She hadn't seen her ex since that night at the restaurant when he demanded that she leave with him and never see Max again.

Kev gestured toward the table. "Mind if I take a seat?"

She blinked a few times, then nodded. He looked different somehow. While he still had the same haircut and she recognized the clothes he wore, there was simply something about him that made her curious. "Sure."

He pulled out the chair, offering her a small smile. "Honestly, I didn't think you'd say yes. Now I don't know what to say."

She chuckled. "I take it that you had a speech planned if I told you to leave me alone?"

Chagrined, Kev looked away. "Maybe."

"I suppose you could start there. Just skip ahead a little bit."

Kev brought his focus back to Ava, then placed his clasped hands on the table. He fiddled with his thumbs as he squirmed in his seat. "I wanted to tell you I was sorry."

Her brows shot up of their own accord. If she had been

asked to guess what Kev would say to her the first time they saw each other after their breakup, it wouldn't have been *that*. But then, Kev didn't seem like himself, either, so she didn't know what she should have expected.

He shifted uncomfortably and his face flushed. "I know you probably won't believe me, and I don't blame you. When we were together ..." He glanced at her then tore his eyes away from her. "When we were together, I didn't treat you the way you deserved."

She sucked in a deep breath and released it slowly. "Kev—"

He held up a hand. "Let me finish. I don't expect you to forgive me either. But I was hoping that you might give me a chance to make it up to you—maybe you would allow us to start over."

She shook her head. "This is all very sweet—and I want you to know how much I appreciate it. But I'm dating someone else."

Ava reached for his hand, unsure if it was instinct or habit. She gave him a small smile. What more could she say? She'd made her choice and it appeared they were both better off because of it.

"Who?"

"I'm sorry?"

"Do I know him?" Kev murmured, withdrawing his hand from her grasp.

She blushed. Out of everything he might have asked, that was the last thing she wanted to answer. What if it triggered him? What if it set him back from the obvious progress he'd been making? She wasn't sure she wanted to be the cause of that.

"It's that friend of yours, isn't it?"

Ava looked away.

"I knew it. From the second I met that guy, I knew he would be trouble."

"Trouble?" she let out a dry laugh. "He's not trouble. He's ... actually, he's pretty amazing. He's giving me the opportunity to start a catering business. He's pushing me to be more—to dream bigger."

"Sounds like he's a bit of a control freak."

"What?" She clasped her hands tightly in her lap. "No, he's not."

"Really? I've known you for ages and you never wanted to try ... what is it? Cooking?"

"Catering," she said.

"Sure. So he waltzes into your life and pressures you to do something you don't want to do. Are there any other issues you have with him?"

Ava wasn't about to spill their most recent argument. Max's decision to keep his mother out of his life was a definite sore spot.

"See? There it is." Kev waved a finger up and down in front of her face. "I can see it in your eyes. There's that disappointment that I spent so much time avoiding. You know I'm right. He's not perfect. No one is."

"You might be right, but perfection isn't what we're supposed to be looking for in a person. Relationships wouldn't ever survive if we had to base everything on that fact alone."

"No, but you broke up with me because you said *I* was controlling. Seems to me that you jumped from one toad to the next. Where's your Prince Charming, Ava?"

"I never said he was my Prince Charming." Now her second thoughts were gaining speed. At one point she had thought that being with Max was exactly where she was supposed to be, but Kev was right that Max had pushed her to do something she was uncomfortable with. But to be fair, it had turned out to be exactly what she wanted. He had refused to listen to her side on that and other issues.

Kev touched her hand briefly, forcing her to shift her attention back to him. "I'm not telling you that you should break up with him."

"Really? Because it sounds like that is exactly what you're trying to do."

"I'm just suggesting that you should think really hard about why you're with him. Men don't change."

She snorted. "Sure seems like you've done a decent job of turning things around."

He pressed his lips together. "That's fair. But with me, it's different. I was able to acknowledge that I was in the wrong. I got help. Do you honestly think Max would go to a therapist to work on himself?"

"You went to a therapist?"

Kev chuckled. "That's beside the point." He got to his feet and stared down at her with the kindest expression she'd ever seen on his face. "It was nice to see you again, Ava. And if you're ever available to hang out again—or go on a date, I'd love it if you gave me a second chance." He rapped his knuckles on the table then slipped away, leaving her alone with her dismal thoughts.

What if Kev was right about Max? Did she really want to spend the rest of her life with someone who would only disregard her feelings on important issues? A little voice reminded her that she had been pushy about his own feelings when it came to his mother.

Ava shut her eyes tight, fighting the emotion that threatened to escape. She couldn't cry in the coffee shop—especially when she had to get back to work in five minutes. The last thing she wanted was to scare off all the customers with red-rimmed eyes.

Her stomach tossed and turned. Maybe she could leave

early due to feeling sick. At least then she'd be able to hide away in her dark apartment and think about all the reasons Kev was wrong.

Because he was.

Still, the more she thought about it, the more unsure she became. Was she doing the right thing with her catering gig? What if no one hired her after she was done with the event? Just because she was going to showcase her cookies at the charity gala didn't mean people would search her out.

Her heart started beating a little harder. Her breaths came out in puffs and her head pounded. She'd been through this before. It was the start of a panic attack. She wasn't sure she was doing the right thing. If her catering thing failed then she'd end up with nothing.

Ava had invested her time and a lot of her savings to do this and all because Max pushed her to. She put her head in her hands trying to figure out what she should do. Max wouldn't let her back out. She knew that much already. And she didn't want to let him down. Either way she'd be paid well for her efforts and she could put that money toward her future, whatever it ended up being.

But she did want to be a baker. She knew that. He was trying to help, she attempted to remind herself.

Still, she couldn't catch her breath. Negative thoughts continued to swirl around her mind. She needed to get some fresh air, but when would she have time to do that? She was supposed to get back to her shift in five minutes.

"Ava? You okay?"

Her head snapped up and she found Izzie staring at her with a deep concern.

"You're really pale. Are you sick?" She glanced up and toward the counter. "Should I tell your boss? Do you need to go home?"

She shook her head vehemently, gulping in the oxygen that had been so hard to catch. "I'm fine."

"You really don't look fine."

"I'm just dealing with a lot right now. You know, getting ready for that charity event and stuff."

Her friend didn't look convinced. If anything, she appeared to be seriously considering going over Ava's head and doing what she wanted on her own.

Just one more person who thought they could make decisions for her.

"Will you guys stop ignoring what I'm saying? When I tell you I'm fine, I mean it. Just ... let me deal with things my way."

Izzie's expression of surprise morphed into something that resembled hurt.

Ava didn't have time to feel guilty. Her friends and family needed to butt out. Once they did, then she would have enough space to do things right. She pushed past her friend and headed behind the counter. Her shift would be over in a few hours. Then she'd go home, get some much-needed rest and decide what to do next.

Chapter Twenty-One

Max paced in front of the door to Ava's home, growing more antsy by the second. He wasn't certain what had happened, and that was mostly Ava's fault.

Why wouldn't she pick up his phone calls?

Their little argument wasn't a big deal. He'd put his foot down and she had to accept that. He wasn't going to do something just because she thought he needed to. And now that his mother was on the same page, Ava couldn't say a single thing about his decision.

When Bart had called him earlier, he started second guessing himself.

Bartholomew Brown was the kind of guy who supported nearly every charity event that Max organized. As such, they were closer than most of the people in the area. And when Bart's wife, Izzie, told him about Ava, of course he would call to check in.

The only thing he got out of them was that Ava looked sick at work and refused to leave. Max had been in meetings all day, so he couldn't stop by the coffee shop to check on her.

But that didn't stop him from calling and messaging her at any spare second he got.

He'd even had his secretary reach out.

But Ava had remained radio silent.

Max tightened and released his fists. The second she showed up, he was going to give her a piece of his mind. They might have had a disagreement, but that didn't mean she could ignore him.

He pulled out his phone to check the time and muttered to himself. If she didn't show up in the next five minutes, he was going to call the police.

Okay, perhaps he wouldn't go that far, but he was going to do something to make it clear to her where they stood.

Then right at that moment, a car pulled into the driveway. Ava got out, locked the doors then trudged toward the house. There was no chance that she hadn't seen him, and yet she didn't look up to meet his eyes as she passed him.

Max reached for her hand, stopping her and forcing her to face him. He searched her eyes, waiting for her to respond to him. But all he got was her fidgeting and looking away. "Ava," he demanded, "what's going on?"

"I don't really want to talk to you right now." She pulled away from him and grabbed her keys.

He watched her fumble with the house key until she finally got it shoved into the lock and turned the knob. She slipped inside and he hurried forward to stop her from shutting him out. She briefly gave him a disgruntled look before she gave up and allowed him to follow her into her home.

Max pushed the door shut behind him and not for the first time, he was worried. This unease was different than earlier. While he'd been concerned for her welfare when he'd gotten the call from Bart, he hadn't thought that there was anything irreparable between the two of them when it came to their relationship.

Ava moved farther into the house with quick steps. Should he follow her? Wait for her to come back out and speak to him? Ava probably hadn't had a good day.

He made his way through the house and ended up in the kitchen doorway. Ava had a cupboard open and she'd pulled out a glass. Her eyes flicked over to him but only briefly before she let out a sigh. "I told you I don't want to talk to you."

"Is this about what happened a few days ago?" Max crossed his arms, waiting for her to respond. If there was anything he knew she hated, it was him making assumptions—even if those assumptions were correct.

Ava filled her glass with water, then moved toward the table. She took a sip, placed the cup on the table then shot him a look.

"Well?"

"Yeah, sorta."

"Sorta? What does that mean?"

"It means that there's a lot going on and when you refuse to listen to me on something, I feel like you don't care about my opinion."

Max stiffened. "Of course I care about your opinion. I think you're very smart."

"Then why on earth wouldn't you just believe me when I tell you that your relationship with your mother is more important than the grudge you're holding?" she shot at him with exasperation.

"So it is about our conversation," he mumbled. "I'm sorry, but you're wrong."

She let out a bark of laughter and shook her head. "See, that's exactly what I mean. I'll tell you how I feel about something and then you disregard it."

"Yeah? Like with what? Because the only thing I can think about is the issue with my mom. Which, for the record, has been resolved in a way both of us want."

THE COOKIE MATCH

Ava blinked at him, disbelief flooding her expression. "You talked to her?"

"Yeah. And she's just as fed up with me as I am with her. We're going our separate ways."

Her face flushed and she pushed away from the table to start pacing. "You weren't supposed to ruin your relationship with her. You're supposed to fix it. I don't believe for one second that she would want you to completely cut ties with her."

"I don't know what to tell you. That's what she said." He shrugged. "Now it's your turn."

"My turn for what?" she demanded.

"Tell me where else I've failed."

She worried her lower lip, hesitating.

"Just say it."

Ava crossed her arms. "You push me when I tell you I don't want to do something."

He frowned. "What are you talking about?"

"The catering. I told you over and over—Nana, too—that I didn't want to do it, I didn't want to get into something I wasn't ready for."

He was speechless. She'd been so excited about the prospect. "I don't know where this is coming from," he murmured. "It's coming out of left field."

She huffed. "Oh, come on. You can't tell me that you haven't seen it. This is what you do. You push and push at me, but when *you* don't want to do something you push back. Can't you see just how hypocritical that is?"

Still, her accusations didn't make sense. They had been in a good place. Everything was on track for the charity event. She had only been upset about his mother. Max dragged a hand down his face and let out a groan. "I'm sorry, I just don't understand where you're getting this. Are you scared? Is that it? Are you worried it's not going to work out—"

"No, it's not because I'm scared, Max. It's because I am worried you're just as controlling as Kev—"

His chest constricted. "Kev? As in the guy who told you we couldn't hang out that one time? You can't seriously be comparing me to *that* guy."

Her hands were now resting on her hips and her stance was more assertive. "He's not the same person he was."

"You saw him? And you didn't tell me?" It was impossible to keep the accusation from seeping into his words.

"I'm sorry? Since when do I have to tell you who I grab a cup of coffee with?"

"This is different and you know it," he growled.

"How is that, exactly?"

"Because he was once your boyfriend."

She threw her hands into the air and let out a derisive laugh. "Oh, so that's where you draw the line. I can't have a conversation with an ex-boyfriend. Emphasis on ex."

"Okay, fine. Go ahead. Clearly, you're trying to tell me that I'm falling short, right? Prove it. Let's get this all out on the table and clear the air. I won't have a relationship with my mother. I won't apologize for encouraging you to chase after a dream I know you're capable of. And now I'm the type to get jealous. Anything else?"

Ava glowered at him, her defenses had surrounded her and she wasn't about to give up. He could see it in the fire behind her eyes. Max should have just left well enough alone, but he couldn't. Right here, right now, he needed to make a point.

"No? Well, how about it's my turn. You refuse to push yourself, your self-motivation is non-existent. You stick your nose in everyone else's business when they don't want to hear it. And you can't make up your mind."

"What are you talking about?"

"I'm talking about me. I'm talking about our relationship. You can't tell me you're not having second thoughts. It's written all over your face. And all it took was one little cup of coffee with your controlling ex. And don't you try to tell me that he's changed. Anyone can pretend to be a better person for thirty minutes."

"Yeah? How about you prove it!" Her voice rose and her face blushed bright red. She was breathing heavier now, and her hands shook.

He blinked, the steam that had been building up inside him dissipating as he took note of her physical appearance. She didn't look so great. In fact, if they kept this up, he wouldn't have been surprised to see her passed out on the floor.

"Well? Show me. Be a better person for thirty minutes," she wheezed.

Max held up his hands. "Ava ... you need to take a deep breath."

"Don't tell me what to do!" She snapped. "I don't need a coach. I don't need someone who only sees me for my potential."

"I never—"

She held up a hand, her eyes darkening. "I want you to leave."

"Ava—"

"Now, Max."

He couldn't move. This wasn't what he'd wanted. Was he angry about Kev manipulating her? Of course. But it wasn't something worth getting this worked up over.

"I mean it, Max. I need you to leave."

Max moved toward her slowly, his hands up as if he were approaching a wild animal, which she might as well have been. "You don't understand. I think we should talk this out."

"We've talked enough."

"That isn't fair—"

She pointed toward the door. "Just go. Please." Her voice

broke and her eyes watered. Before a tear was able to slip down her cheek she squeezed her eyes shut and turned away.

"Ava."

"I'll still do the charity gala, but I don't want to see you anymore."

Max watched her, praying that she might suddenly change her mind and tell him she'd give him a chance to talk—to listen to her. But she didn't. The room got several degrees colder. He wasn't going to get a second chance. He knew her well enough to understand that perfectly.

He'd lost the two people closest to him in the course of one day.

Chapter Twenty-Two

The weeks without seeing or hearing from Max were excruciating. At first, Ava didn't think she could handle it. He'd been her cheerleader when she didn't think she could handle the pressure.

Yes, he was the one responsible for said pressure, but he was also there reminding her every step of the way that she could do it.

"You're doing great."

Her head snapped up and she met Peter's discerning gaze. She'd almost forgotten he was here with her, using the kitchen at Maple Gardens to prepare what he needed to bring to the table—both literally and figuratively.

She gave him a tentative smile. Never in her life had she felt so inadequate. She'd been safe behind the counter at the coffee shop. It had been a good job, one where she didn't have to think too hard—and definitely one without high stakes.

Peter nodded as if he could hear her thoughts and he wanted to reassure her that he meant what he said.

"Thanks," she mumbled. "Sometimes I worry that we'll

get there for this event and I'm going to fail so miserably that you're going to be brought down with me."

Peter laughed. "Boy, that got dark quick."

She flushed and turned her focus to the macarons she was filling. "Sorry."

"Don't be. I've been where you are."

She glanced at him again, surprised.

"It's true. I've been working here for so long that I started seeing myself as someone who was only capable of putting together a menu for the residents. Don't get me wrong, I love doing that. But I started to doubt my ability to create dishes for people who expect stellar creations."

Her heart dropped to her stomach. She hadn't even been thinking about impressing the people. She'd been stuck on the possibility of ruining the food, not making enough, or some other catastrophic issue.

Now she could add falling short of the expectations of others to her list of things to stress about.

"That's why I'm not going to do anything else after this. I'm going back to the coffee shop. That's where I belong."

Peter gave her a strange kind of look. "What are you talking about? You can't do that."

"Oh yes, I can. You're starting to sound like Max."

Peter wiped his hands on a dish towel and flung it over his shoulder. "When you were in elementary school and you passed addition, you moved on to subtraction, right?"

She laughed. "I guess so."

"And when you started on your subtraction, you weren't as good. You stumbled, got a lot of questions wrong, but you couldn't just give up and go back to doing only addition."

Ava put down her decorating bag. "I don't know what you're getting at."

"Well, when you do an event like this, you can't just go back to doing addition. It's going to be boring—too easy."

"What if I want easy? What if I'm exhausted from all this hustle and it's not something I enjoy anymore?"

"Well, is it?"

She snapped her mouth shut.

Even in Max's absence, she'd enjoyed making these cookies, experimenting with the last few recipes before she started making them in bulk. It was easy to get lost in the craft. Peter had made a good point. "See? There it is. I can tell those cogs are whirling. You know exactly what I'm talking about."

"I don't know," she murmured.

"Don't let your fear of the unknown hold you back from following your dreams. Take it from me, that's no life worth living." He flashed her a smile then headed into the walk-in refrigerator.

What he said sounded suspiciously like something Max might tell her, but she knew better than to assume Peter was getting his cues from Max. Max had kept his distance, even to the extent that she hadn't seen his name on the visitor logs—not even to see his mother. That little bit of information really saddened her. She still hoped that one day Max and Lily would find a way to reconcile.

Ava grabbed her pastry bag and started back to work. She didn't like the combination of feelings that were overwhelming her.

She didn't want to think about Max or the way his absence made her feel. She didn't like realizing that Max might have had a point about her following her dreams. To hear someone else bring logic to a point where her heart fought against it was very uncomfortable.

The feelings continued to build until she couldn't handle being in the kitchen.

Ava tossed down her bag, tore off her apron and hurried out of the kitchen. The hallway was quiet, devoid of visitors and residents alike. She'd only been here a handful of times, and never to visit the residents.

The first time she'd come, Peter had shown her what she had to use at her disposal. So when she found herself outside in the beautiful gardens, she was thrown off guard. She stopped and crumpled over, placing her hands on her knees as she took in deep breaths.

There was something wrong with her if she couldn't even handle thinking about Max and her job without losing her cool. If anything provided proof that she needed to step back, it was this.

When she finally straightened, she was able to fully appreciate the scenery around her. Trees dotted the landscape, shading large areas and several wrought-iron benches. There was a path that wound lazily around a fountain and was probably designed to encourage the residents to get some exercise.

All in all, this place was lovely. It wasn't any wonder that Lily would have chosen such a place to retire.

Someone bumped into her and she jumped out of the way, mumbling her apology until she got a good look at the woman. Ava would have recognized Lily anywhere.

Lily peered at her, brows creased. Then recognition filled her eyes. "Ava? Is that you?"

Oh, how she wished she could lie and tell this woman that she was mistaken. What wouldn't she give to just spin around and take off running? But that wasn't who she was.

Ava nodded. "Yeah ... yes. It's nice to see you again, Lily."

The older woman's brown eyes crinkled at the corners and her expression brightened. "What are you doing here?" She looked past Ava. "Is Max with you?"

Hot, searing flames burst to life beneath her skin as she shook her head and looked away. "I'm just here to prepare for a charity event he's organizing."

THE COOKIE MATCH

"Oh! I heard about that." She patted Ava's arm. "I knew you would do great things, dear."

"Thank you," Ava murmured, a bit unsure how else to respond.

Lily motioned toward the nearest free bench. "Would you care to visit?"

Glancing toward the bench, Ava nearly declined. She had a lot of work to do, and Max wouldn't be thrilled to discover that they were chatting.

But then that thought alone pushed her forward. If Max wouldn't talk to his mother, then she would. Ava nodded, then followed Lily as she led the way to their seat.

"I wanted to tell you that I think Max is wrong," Ava blurted before her behind hit the seat. She grimaced, hating the way she couldn't keep her nose out of their business. "I lost my mother and I know how important that relationship is—"

Lily placed her hand on Ava's knee. "I'm going to stop you right there, dear. A few weeks ago, I would have agreed with you. But I've realized something. It's no good to force a relationship either. If Max wants to mend things, he'll do so. I can't force him. He's an adult who is capable of making his own decisions."

"But it isn't right."

Lily gave her a patient smile. "All I can do is try to be the kind of person he wants to spend time with. I made some terrible decisions, and I have to suffer the consequences."

"But he's still holding the grudge—"

"His wounds run deep. And that is entirely my fault." She took a deep breath and stared off into the distance. "When I met Max's father, I believed my chance at love had passed by. I wasn't getting any younger. But then this wonderful and handsome gentleman swept me off my feet and I fell head over heels in love."

Lily's eyes shone with the memory, but then, her face dropped.

"All too soon, yet not soon enough, he confessed he was married. He lived in Europe and was in an arranged marriage which was desperately unhappy. I was distraught and sent him away. It broke my heart but then I discovered I was expecting Max."

"Oh my goodness!"

"I made the choice then and there to raise our child alone. It was a decision made out of respect for his wife because no matter how unhappy the marriage, she didn't deserve what he'd done. So Max and I muddled through. Now and then I saw a glimpse of his father on television for he was a wealthy businessman. I learned that his wife had passed away and that they had no heirs."

"Did you ever see him again?"

"Never. He died soon after and it was a terrible shock when I was informed that he'd left me a considerable sum of money. He never knew about Max. They never got to meet."

Ava's heart went out to Lily. She'd lost her great love and then lost Max.

"The other thing... and I am ashamed of this. I did fail to pass on your messages. Max was only just beginning to settle into his new life and I thought he might be pulled back toward the old. He always cared so deeply for you."

"We're no longer dating. It's a long story, but a lot of it has to do with our differences. We just ... don't quite see eye to eye, you know?"

"Max can be rather difficult at times. I suppose I have a lot to do with that." Lily sent a quick glance in Ava's direction before turning her attention outward. "Just ... think about it a little before you give up on him. He's been through a lot. I'm sure he needs you more than he will ever admit to either one of us." Her smile returned and she got to her feet. "It was lovely chatting with you dear. I do hope you'll come around to visit me again." She got to her feet and without another word, wandered away, leaving Ava to contemplate all the new information she'd been given.

Chapter Twenty-Three

Max wasn't in a bad mood. It didn't matter how many people outright told him they thought he was. He'd deny it until he was red in the face. Sometimes relationships didn't work out. And more often than not, they didn't work out between people who were only meant to remain friends.

He should have kept Ava in the friend zone. That would have been the smart thing to do. Now, he didn't have a girlfriend or his best friend.

And *that* was the reason he was working longer hours.

Unfortunately, because he had decided to come in early and stay late, so had Cathy. He'd reminded her that she didn't have to, but she insisted. Now, as the building got dark and only the necessary lights had been left on, the only sounds Max could hear were the clacking of computer keys just outside his office door.

If he were honest with himself, he would just admit how miserable he was being unable to see Ava regularly.

Funnily enough, Max had never thought he had a lot of it to begin with. Only now, he'd realized just how wrong he was. He stared at the neat stack of paperwork that sat on his desk.

THE COOKIE MATCH

He'd completed everything early and it had been a stretch to find other things to keep him busy.

Going back to his apartment wasn't an option, because it felt even emptier than his office. He didn't want to wander the streets or go to a bar to watch a game. He didn't have any friends he felt he could invite himself over to visit with.

He was alone.

For the first time in his life, he truly felt alone. Once upon a time he'd felt like his life held meaning. He could see the path he was supposed to take clear as day. Every night he went to bed feeling complete and fulfilled.

How had losing someone who'd only recently come back into his life been able to do so much damage to his psyche?

"Thinking about her again?"

Max's head lifted from the stack of papers and he found Cathy standing in the doorway watching him with a thoughtful expression. She gave him a small smile, leaning her shoulder against the door. He wasn't sure how long she'd been watching him or how she'd managed to figure out that he had broken things off with Ava, but at this point he should just be grateful he didn't have to explain anything.

This was why he'd hired her. Cathy was good at what she did because she was observant.

"You don't have to talk about it," Cathy murmured as she moved into the room. "I know guys don't usually like to talk about that sort of thing. But maybe it would do you some good to get out of the office and get your mind off it."

He shook his head. "I'm busy—"

She laughed, taking a seat in the chair that faced his desk. "I have your schedule. I know what you have to get done and when."

Max wasn't sure if it was out of habit or because of the growing regret, but he stiffened when Cathy mentioned his mother. Ava had a strong opinion about that situation and there was no telling what Cathy thought of his decision to steer clear of his mother at this time.

"Anyway, as I was saying, I think you need to get out. Do something you enjoy. What are your interests?"

He glanced at the paperwork on the desk again.

"Interests that don't include work. For as long as I have known you, there hasn't been a single day when you weren't putting in one hundred and ten percent. You're more like the Energizer Bunny than a man." Cathy let out a laugh. "And the sad part is that you're one of the most eligible bachelors in this town. You're smart, handsome, and you've got money. You could have your pick of women." This time she flushed, looking away from him. "I'm sorry if that wasn't appropriate for me to say, but it's true."

Those were all things he had heard before from various people—men and women alike. He'd been interviewed by news and radio where the questions ranged from when was he going to find a nice young woman and settle down. He'd never been able to come up with an answer to satisfy the interviewers, mostly because he didn't have any interest in settling down.

Until Ava came back into his life.

He needed to stop those thoughts right now.

Ava wasn't an option. They couldn't see eye to eye on several issues and neither one of them was willing to compromise. It would be unwise for them to try to reconcile. He needed to find someone else.

"You need to find someone who understands you."

His eyes snapped to meet hers. Had he said any of that out loud? No. Cathy was just really good at her job. Even still, her ability to read him so easily had a way of unsettling him. He stared at her long enough that she started to fidget in her seat.

"Anyway … I was thinking, if you were interested, maybe you'd consider …" She looked away then lifted her hand to tuck her hair behind her ear. "You can say no if you'd like. I don't know if it's against the rules or anything ..." This time Cathy let out a strangled laugh. "Will you go out with me?"

He straightened in his seat. Ava had been right. She'd seen that Cathy was interested in him and he'd always suspected the same. He found himself wondering just how long she'd been watching him, waiting for him to get the hint.

His company didn't have specific rules about dating a coworker, but this was somewhat different. He was her boss. The power dynamic could be construed as being a problem.

Then again, she was the one who asked him out. One date wouldn't hurt, would it? He could accept her request and they could have a nice night.

It would be a relief to do something to take his mind off Ava.

"I'm so sorry. I shouldn't have asked—" Cathy scrambled to her feet, her face cherry red.

He shot up from his chair and held out a hand. "I think that sounds nice." He'd allowed himself to get inside his own head, when she'd been waiting for him to answer and now he probably appeared to be accepting her offer because he felt bad. "What did you have in mind?"

She didn't look convinced. As she stood there, practically having one foot out the door, he had to do something to ease the tension.

"Dinner? Dancing? Bowling? What do you like to do on a Friday night?"

Cathy's lips lifted somewhat. "I've loved dancing since I was a teenager. I know this great place about fifteen minutes from here."

He nodded as he walked around his chair and pushed it in. "Let's do it."

❄

Flashing lights filled the room, while the floor vibrated with beats from the music. From the outside, this place looked like a nightclub where folks would come to hide away in dark corners to be intimate with someone. But as soon as they got inside, Max realized he was wrong.

This was the kind of club where people came to *really* dance. Salsa, mambo, the waltz, all kinds of ballroom styles. There were a share of couples spending time away from the dance floor to be together, but for the most part, everyone was enjoying the fast pace of the music and moving across the room like they were on clouds.

"Isn't this place great?" Cathy leaned in closer but still had to yell.

"I didn't realize this place existed," he called back.

"Come on." She grabbed his hand and pulled him onto the dance floor.

"I only know the basics," he resisted at first, but when they collided and she wrapped her hands around his neck, he asked himself why he was fighting this so much.

"Just let everything go and feel the music. Don't worry about tomorrow or yesterday. Just think about what's happening right here, right now. That's all you have to do."

Her words had a strange effect on him. He wanted to believe her, to let go and forget all about what he'd had ... what he'd lost. Cathy's words made sense. When something went wrong, it was better to move on.

So that was what he was determined to do.

At least for tonight.

They danced every song for the first half hour and he could pretend that he was perfectly fine. But toward the end of those thirty minutes, he was hit hard. People weren't anything without their pasts. Their mistakes, their achievements—they were the sum total of what made a person who they were. And just like that, he saw flashes of everything that filled him with gut-wrenching shame.

The relationship with his mother came first. It hit him over the head so hard he had to stop mid-step to catch his breath. He held up a hand when Cathy opened her mouth, presumably to ask him what was wrong. Max shook his head, swallowing to push down a lump in his throat.

Max ducked out of the building and onto the sidewalk out front. He leaned against the wall and let his head fall back, touching the rough brick. Shutting his eyes, he felt the emotion bubble up. First it felt like it was happening in slow motion, then all at once it washed over him.

Guilt for what he'd put his mother through. When he was younger he would ask and ask to know more about his father and Lily had only ever said that he'd been a good man in a difficult situation. Then when she wanted to talk about his father, Max had refused to listen, as if making his mother feel bad would ease his own pain.

He was a stubborn fool who should have realized what he had been doing way before now.

His whole body heated uncomfortably with this realization. Not only that, his stomach twisted and knotted. The nausea that swirled along the knots made his legs go numb.

This was what it really felt like to be on the wrong side of a burned bridge. Here he was, alone and wondering how he was going to fix what he'd broken. Was there even a chance he could?

"Max?" Cathy's quiet voice dragged him from the pits where he'd landed and he glanced in her direction.

She stood with her hands clutched tightly in front of her, a look of disappointment in her eyes.

"Are you okay?"

He shook his head. It was probably the first honest thing he'd done since his argument with his mother. He couldn't even bring himself to tell her that he had made a mistake in coming out with her. The longer he was out here, the more he couldn't stop thinking about Ava.

Or about his mother.

"I probably shouldn't have asked you out tonight." She gave him a small smile. "Can't blame a girl for trying."

Max took in a deep breath. He worked his jaw then forced a smile. "For what it's worth, it was nice to get out. What you said on the dance floor resonated and I've just done some serious thinking about my future. Made me realize a few truths, one of which is how much I love Ava."

"I might go back inside. There was a nice guy who just asked me to dance and now that I've helped my boss," she said with a grin. "It might be time to take my own advice." Cathy let herself back inside.

Now, Max needed to figure out how to fix everything—and hopefully before the event in two weeks.

With his mother.

And with Ava.

Chapter Twenty-Four

Nothing could have prepared Ava for what she would encounter at her first catering event. This wasn't anything like serving coffee to the folks who came in to *Just Peachy*.

Every person who entered the ballroom was dressed to the nines. Ava watched from the window of the swinging kitchen door as the tables filled up. She couldn't find a single person who looked like they didn't belong. She hadn't seen Max arrive yet, and she'd been expecting that he would have been one of the first.

Behind her, Peter was dishing out commands to the team that Max had hired for them. From cooks to servers, they had an army that would only make them shine. Ava did one more sweep of the banquet room for the host of the charity event but had zero luck.

It wasn't like she even knew what she would say to him. The way they had left things had almost made her not want to show tonight. But she knew better than to bail. She'd been here for the last two hours prepping and already she could tell she loved this part of the business.

Being involved in running the kitchen gave her a rush. She

had only gotten a spare moment to check for Max when she was called back over to her station.

"Take those cookies out with the champagne. We want everyone to whet their appetites not only with something savory, but with something sweet." She directed the order to a young man who quickly grabbed the tray she'd prepared for the start of the party.

Ava watched him head off and glanced over toward Peter who looked just as swamped as ever—but also as happy as she was. He must have felt her staring because he turned his eyes in her direction, then grinned. He nodded at her and she did the same.

The whirlwind continued in the kitchen but every so often she'd catch a glimpse of what was happening out at the party. Music played, guests chatted, and the air felt utterly electrifying. While Peter oversaw the plating of the meals, Ava focused on doing the same with her dessert dishes.

There were a few moments when she was so caught up in the excitement that she wanted someone to talk to.

Not just anyone.

Max.

If she wasn't careful, she would allow herself to get pulled under and dragged down by the ache of his absence. Their argument had stung harder than she'd like to admit. With how close they'd been when they were younger, and how close they'd recently become, this loss felt harder than she thought it would be.

Emotion burned behind her eyes as she sprinkled some powdered sugar on the crème brûlée cookies. They blurred and she had to blink to clear up her vision. As much as she wanted to blame him completely for their fight, she couldn't.

Deep down, Ava knew Max was a good man. He'd shown it time and time again. If she judged him in his moments of weakness, then she'd be a hypocrite. Everyone had bad days—

some were worse than others. The talk with Lily had done much to help her understand Max more, even if it was too late for them.

Ava took a step back and admired her work, wiping her hands on a nearby towel. That final touch was the last thing she needed to complete. She gestured for the waiters to take the plates out. Peter sidled up beside her, leaning against the island where she'd been working. "We did it."

She smiled back, half-heartedly. "Yeah. We did it."

He gestured toward the door. "Do you want to head out there and catch the end of it?"

On the one hand, she longed to see Max again, to see him in his element. She wanted to tell him that she should have been more supportive of him and his feelings. But something she couldn't put her finger on held her back. "I don't know if that's a good idea."

"Why not? I'm sure Max will be thanking the catering team at the end of the auction. I've heard he does that at most of his events." Peter nudged her. "Come on. Even if he doesn't highlight our work, it's nice to see people appreciating the food you made." Peter backed away and moved toward the door, before stopping and shooting one more look toward her. "Coming?"

Ava glanced at the door that would take her to where Max was. He'd likely come back to tell Peter thanks for his work. And she didn't want them to be at odds forever.

Would they ever get back to where they were before? She couldn't be sure. But she would like to become friends again. And after tonight, she knew where she wanted to go with her baking talent.

A cookie shop sounded so much better than the coffee place where she was currently working. She heaved a sigh and nodded. "Okay, but you can't leave my side and we have to stay in the back where no one can see us."

He chuckled. "Whatever you say."

They slipped out into the ballroom and along the wall until they found a good place to watch the auction. Not a single table had an empty seat. The servers were coming and going with the desserts now that they had cleared the table from the dinner.

An auctioneer rattled on about a piece of jewelry on display and various people held up signs to bid. Ava had never been to an event quite like this one. Even though she'd gotten a good look at everything before it began, seeing it in full swing was like going to a theme park for the first time.

She couldn't focus on just one thing.

That was when she saw them. Near the front and in the center was a table filled with familiar women. They were dressed just as nicely as the rest of the guests and their hair and makeup had been done as well. Ava stared at the table, confusion flooding every sense. There were three women she recognized as residents of Maple Gardens. But the biggest surprise was who was right there in what Ava considered to be the best seat.

Lily Stone.

Nearby at another table were a few of the staff members from Maple Gardens.

Peter chuckled and Ava swung her eyes toward him, suddenly realizing that her mouth was hanging open. "I take it you didn't know that Max had a table set up just for his mother and her friends."

She returned her gaze to the table, noting just how happy these women were to be here and part of the action. Ava shook her head, reminding herself to shut her mouth, so she didn't look quite so ridiculous. "I had no idea."

Peter smiled, his arms crossed as he shifted his weight to lean against the wall. "Yeah, I couldn't quite believe it myself when Quinne told me. She was ecstatic when she found out.

It's been a long time since her mother has been able to get out and do something like this."

Ava couldn't believe it either. The last time she'd spoken to Max, he'd told her that his mother had cut ties with him and that both of them were happy where things ended up.

Of course, that had been wrong. She'd been able to see right through it. Or rather, she knew that he'd regret doing it. She just hadn't thought he'd come full circle so soon. Her heart burst with warmth and a tingling sensation dragged its way to all of her extremities.

But that pride she felt over Max's change of heart was short-lived. What if they had only brought out the worst in each other?

Her heart constricted, turning cold, and she shivered. The sounds from the party seemed to be so far off, now. If she was right, then this would only add to all of the evidence stacked against her.

Every relationship she'd had over the last decade had ended terribly.

What if *she* was the problem, somehow?

She pressed her lips between her teeth and bit down hard to keep herself from letting out the whimper that threatened to escape. Whatever it was about her that brought out the worst in these men wasn't good at all. The worst part was that she didn't know what it was. How could she change things if she didn't know what was wrong?

"Hey," she mumbled, turning toward Peter, "I think I'm going to duck out for some fresh air."

Peter looked concerned. "Are you feeling sick?"

"I'm just a little lightheaded. I think I overextended myself. But if you think you can handle things from here—" She really needed to escape before Max made his appearance. Her heart couldn't take seeing him again after everything—

especially after seeing how much he'd grown over the last few weeks.

"How's everyone doing tonight?"

The blood drained from Ava's face when she heard his voice. That warm, husky voice that could send shivers down her spine was exactly what she'd wanted to avoid. Slowly, she turned her head and her legs nearly buckled beneath her.

Maximus Stone stood on stage, bathed in lights, and dressed like he was ready to get married. He had never looked more attractive than he did in that moment—and all dismal thoughts of what had happened between them faded.

"Thank you all for coming out for this event. As most of you know, this charity is something I hold close to my heart. Children are so important to our future—and making sure they are loved and cared for is the foundation of giving them the best chance in life." Max's eyes landed on Ava. If she had thought she could slip out, she was dead wrong. There would be no escape tonight, not with the way he'd just locked her in her place. "There will be plenty of time to talk about my charity. First, I'd like to shine a spotlight on two very important people. Ava Brooks and Peter Edmonds. Without them, your plates would have been empty. Can we get a round of applause for these amazing chefs!" His arm swung out in her direction and with it several heads.

Applause shook the room then faded into oblivion as Max's eyes continued to pin her to her place. A whole conversation passed between them during those cheers. Her heart practically split in two.

Well, this was just great.

What was she supposed to do now?

Chapter Twenty-Five

Even in her catering uniform, Ava looked beautiful. Max had watched her from across the room from the second she entered the ballroom with Peter. It took every ounce of his mental strength to not just march through the tables, chairs, and guests so he could speak to her.

Unfortunately, he was due on stage and what he had to say to her would take longer than that.

Max gripped the podium so tightly his fingertips turned white. He prayed she'd stay put long enough for him to take her aside and tell her how wrong he'd been. There was a great deal of risk in such a confession.

She might not believe him.

Silence dragged him from his thoughts, and he turned his focus out to the crowd. He glanced down at the table right in front of him and he met his mother's gaze. She smiled, nodded, and that was all it took to get him back on track. "I've had to do some soul-searching lately when it came to my own family. It took me too long to realize that, with so many children out there without families, one should nurture the family you do have."

His eyes flitted over to Ava, if only to assure himself that she was still there. On confirming that, he let his focus sweep through the crowd. "Families are the ones who should love you no matter what. I've made my fair share of mistakes over the years. But I've realized something recently. Holding a grudge doesn't teach anyone anything." He met his mother's gaze once more. "Communication, willingness to listen, and an open heart? Now that is a way forward."

He'd paused to gather his thoughts and to contain his emotions, but it was long enough of one that the crowd burst with applause once more. He nodded, forcing a smile as he held up his hands to quiet the crowd. "I never had a chance to meet my father. Some of the children we help have struggled with something similar. Your contributions tonight will aid in our efforts to reunite children who are looking for their parents. The children might have aged out of the foster system or simply want to connect with their blood relatives, but they deserve to know their family as much as any of us."

Max continued the speech he'd prepared, and wrapped everything up by touching briefly on his relationship with his mother, and then thanking everyone for their generosity. When he concluded, the crowd clapped and cheered. Music resumed, as well as quiet chatter. His eyes shifted toward the wall where Ava had been standing and his heart bottomed out.

She was gone.

His eyes swept through the crowd, darting back and forth as he hustled from the stage like a zombie. It was a miracle he didn't snap his neck on his way down the steps. She couldn't have left. She had to stick around to clean up, right?

Then again, what did he know? She might have worked out a deal with Peter on clean-up.

That thought alone was enough to propel him through the crowd and toward the swinging doors of the kitchen. He wasn't sure what would happen if she managed to take off before he had a chance to talk to her. For all he knew, she'd find a way for him to stay out of her life for good. He wasn't dumb enough to believe his little speech would be enough to win her over, though it had been a good start.

His mouth went dry. His limbs were numb. Each person who stepped into his path to congratulate him on another successful gala tore at his patience little by little. If he didn't get to Ava before she took off, he wasn't sure he'd be able to handle another polite conversation with any of these people.

When he finally burst into the kitchen, the swinging doors thumping against one another, he stopped only long enough to search through the folks he'd startled for a familiar pair of eyes.

Ava wasn't in here. She hadn't been in the ballroom either.

"Ms. Brooks?" he asked the nearest server.

The young woman's head whipped around to glance through the kitchen. "I'm sorry. I haven't seen her."

He didn't imagine she'd slip out the main entrance. If she was still here, she would have gone out the back. It was his only shot to catch her.

With quick steps, Max hurried toward the back and out the heavy metal door that led to the stairs. He galloped down the concrete steps, turning corners far too quickly, nearly skidding into the wall, then headed down the next row of stairs.

When he finally got to the bottom, he threw himself out of the doors. The cool, humid, night air hit him. Traffic roared on the busy roads nearby. Laughter from a couple passing on the sidewalk. But there was no sign of Ava.

His chest heaved, but whether from the exertion of running down those stairs or because he'd lost his shot with the girl of his dreams, the reason was a toss-up.

Max's shoulders drooped. He ran a rough hand down his

face, attempting to rein in his disappointment. He wasn't going to give up. He couldn't.

Ava was worth fighting for.

"Max?"

He froze.

"Max? What are you doing out here?" Ava's quiet voice came from behind him.

Slowly he turned around.

She leaned against the brick wall of the building, her arms crossed. Her eyes watched him much like he'd imagine a small deer would keep an eye on a nearby predator. Her nose and cheeks were pink. She looked upset, but there wasn't any sign of tears.

He took a step toward her, then thought better of it. "I needed to talk to you."

Ava glanced toward the door then shook her head. "I don't know if that's a good—"

"You were right."

She swung her focus back to him.

"You were right to believe in the importance of family."

"Max," she sighed. "It was a beautiful speech, but I don't think—"

He took another step toward her. "It wasn't just a speech. It was the truth. I've had a lot of time to think about what I was doing and what held me back and why."

This time she didn't argue. She simply stared at him. He couldn't tell if that was a good thing or a bad thing. At this point, he was just grateful that she was giving him a chance to explain himself.

Max took a deep breath and released it slowly before speaking.

"I've been angry and resentful toward my mother for so long that I couldn't see past the walls I'd built. And then when

THE COOKIE MATCH

I found you again ... or you found me, it broke me to hear that you'd tried to stay in touch. I didn't even see the obvious which was that I had made little effort to remedy that. All I could see were the mistakes of others, not my own. I was wrong to do that."

"Yeah," she mumbled. "You were."

"I'm trying to be better." There was a note of pleading in his voice, but he didn't care. All he wanted was for her to hear him out. At least that was what he kept telling himself.

When she didn't comment, he fought the instinct to become defensive and protect his heart, not when he had come to accept he was in the wrong.

"I'm sorry for what I said. If I could take it all back—"

"But that's just it. You can't. And I can't either. I said horrible things to you." Ava pushed away from the wall and approached him. "Sometimes you can't undo the wrong you caused. That's just the way things are. Sometimes you have to just let things be."

He swallowed down the painful lump her words had caused. He wouldn't have been able to find his voice if he overturned every single stone in a one hundred mile radius. So he listened, he nodded, and he swore to himself that he wasn't going to give up hope.

"But..."

Max's eyes cut to meet hers. "But?"

She pressed her lips together into a thin line. "I have never seen those ladies so happy. I can't believe you got them all dressed up and out for a night on the town." A smile tugged at the corners of her lips. "You either did some major soul-searching, or you knew exactly what to do to get me into listening to you."

He shook his head, moving toward her once more. "I'm not trying to manipulate—"

Ava held up her hand with a small laugh. "Relax, Max, it was a joke. I know you're not trying to manipulate me." Her eyes darted away then came back to meet his. "I think it was really sweet—what you did for your mother. I'm glad you were willing to meet her halfway and talk about your issues so that you could mend what was broken."

Max took a step back, nodding once more. He searched for something—anything to say to her that would keep her talking, but all he could come up with was, "The food was good."

Her smile widened slightly. "Thanks."

"People are raving about it."

"That's good."

He cleared his throat then heaved a heavy breath. "I should probably ..."

Leaving now, on a good note, was the right thing to do. If Ava wanted to see him, then he'd be ready to show her how much he'd changed. She was everything to Max. But he'd put pressure on her in the past over the event and he wasn't going to act that way any longer.

Without another word, he stepped toward the door and pulled it open. The heavy metal clanged as it swiftly shut behind him.

Max put one foot on the bottom step, his hand on the rail, trying to get the courage just to climb the stairs and return to the party without telling Ava how he felt about her—that he was lost without her.

And that all he wanted to do was pull her into his arms and never let go.

His feet felt like they weighed a thousand pounds as he lifted one to the next step.

The door behind him whooshed open and Ava's voice echoed in the stairwell. "Max?"

He lifted his head but didn't turn around.

"Do you think we could get some coffee sometime?"

Max glanced over his shoulder then turned to face her fully. "How about tomorrow?"

She grinned. "Pick me up at nine?"

"I'll be there."

Chapter Twenty-Six

Ava's feet tapped on the floor as she sat in the chair near the window. Max was at the counter ordering their usual, and all she could think about was how well last night had gone.

Several people at the function had requested a meeting with Peter and her and already she had one gig lined up. It was a small one, but thrilling all the same.

She pressed her hands between her knees in an attempt to quell her nervous energy. Max didn't know about the gig, nor did he know that she'd finally come to a decision regarding her future career in the catering industry.

Part of her nervous energy was that she had a favor to ask him. On the one hand, had they not broken up, she wouldn't have worried about asking him for such a favor. But now that they might be giving it another shot, she thought he might think she was just here so she could get his help.

Her face flushed at the thought of asking him for the loan. He had the money. And while she would have never dreamed of asking him for any, even while they were dating, this was a business venture and he would be an investor.

She was nearly ready to ask him, but then he returned to the table and handed her the coffee.

That was when she realized she simply couldn't ask him. It wasn't fair to either of them. She'd just have to find her way on her own.

Max pulled out the chair and smiled at her as he took his seat. Fresh flutters rippled through her body, and she stared down at her coffee. She should be happy. They were finally on a path that made sense.

He was fixing things with his mother. And she was finally going after her dreams. His hand came out of nowhere and grasped hers over the table.

Ava's head snapped up and she peered at him. The tension from the night before had carried over to today, and why wouldn't it? They were starting fresh. Things were bound to be difficult at first.

"I was surprised you wanted to get coffee," he murmured. "But I'm glad you did."

She nodded. "I would be lying if I said I didn't miss you." Ava glanced down to where his hand clasped hers, watching with wonder as he trailed his thumb over her knuckles and enjoying the shiver that accompanied the motion. "I *really* missed you, Max," she rasped.

"I missed you, too."

She smiled, forcing herself to bring her eyes up to meet his once more. "The gala was a success?"

He nodded. "We exceeded every goal."

"That's wonderful."

"And you? Was the event everything that you hoped it would be?"

"More," she murmured. "I can't thank you enough for what you did to get me there. I can't believe it has taken me so long to finally accept this was what I was born to do." Once again, she felt compelled to ask him for his assistance. She knew she could do a lot with a small loan.

But she fought it, clamping her mouth shut and refusing to fall prey to another bad impulse.

"Peter said the two of you got to speak to some of the guests about additional work?"

She glanced up. Of course, Peter would be open about such an opportunity. He was more than capable of continuing the way things were. But if she wanted to expand, she'd need help. Ava swallowed hard, nodding. "Yes. There were a few opportunities."

He chuckled. "Come on, Ava. You're not going to make me drag it out of you, are you?"

Gnawing on her lower lip, she finally succumbed to his request. "I have a gig lined up for the end of the month. They want several dozen cookies for a corporate event."

"That's great!" His enthusiasm warmed her inside and out.

"Yeah, it really is."

"Then why do you seem so ... blasé about the whole thing?"

Ava couldn't meet his gaze. This wasn't what she'd wanted this little date to be. She wanted to start fresh, to see where things could go without the catering gig or the relationship he had with his mother hanging over their heads. "Can we just ... talk about something else?"

The confusion that radiated from him was more than enough to bring on guilt.

"What's the matter, Ava? I thought you wanted this—that everything had been building up to this moment."

She let out a sigh. "It was—*is*." Finally, she let it all out: her excitement, frustration, and everything that came with it. "This is everything that I never knew I wanted. I can see it now, Max. I can see myself running a bakery or a catering business specializing in those cookies I made. I can see people lining up outside of a small shop just so they can order a dozen of their favorite flavor. I want it *all*."

"Okay ..." he drawled, "I'm sorry, but I'm failing to see where there's a problem. And clearly there is or you wouldn't be yelling at me."

She blinked and slapped a hand over her mouth to stifle an embarrassed laugh. "You're right. I'm so sorry!"

Max shook his head. "Don't be. I love seeing this side of you."

"The angry side?" she laughed again, if only to keep her mortification in check.

"No, the passionate one."

This time she couldn't think of a single word to say to him. Passionate. Wasn't he listening? She was a mess.

Max reached for her hand again, somehow having lost hold of it. "I take it you're worried about getting started."

"Yeah," she said, "and a thousand other things."

Suddenly he got to his feet. "Come with me." Max tugged her out of her chair.

"What? Where are we going?"

"You'll see."

"Max," she laughed again, "you can't just say we're going somewhere and not tell me. You could be kidnapping me, and I would like to know whether or not I should be trying to escape."

He rolled his eyes but laughed at the same time. "Will you just trust me for once? I want to show you something."

"But you forgot your coffee." She glanced over her shoulder toward the cup he'd left there.

"This is more important," he insisted.

So she let him guide her out of the coffee shop. Rather than head for his car, he turned down the street and they walked until they had to cross. After turning a corner then crossing the street again, he came to a stop in front of a bookstore.

Ava glanced at the store, lifting one brow. "Let me guess, you think there's a really good book in there on entrepreneurship."

He chuckled, and the sound seemed to slip beneath every defense she'd ever had, knocking them down one by one. He reached out both hands, placed them on her shoulders, then turned her around so she faced the street.

"So you're going to push me in front of traffic now, are you?"

Max came around to stand beside her. He pointed and she turned her head so she was focused on an old, darkened storefront. There was no sign hanging overhead and it looked as though it had been vacant for at least a year. His face came into view, bright and smiling. "Do you like it?"

"I ... don't know what I'm looking at," she hedged.

He waved a hand over the top of them. "Imagine it. A cute lit sign that reads, 'Do it for the Cookies'."

She snorted. Then she gaped at him. "Wait, you're serious."

"I'm deadly serious." This time he came to stand between her and the store. Taking both of her hands in his, he offered her a chagrined smile. "I have always known you would do amazing things. Even when we were kids, I could see the potential you had. You just needed someone to believe in you."

Ava blinked then looked over at the store again. "But ... what ... you're kidding." She shut her eyes then turned her focus to him completely. "Please explain."

"I leased it for the next year." He quirked a wider grin at her. "I tried to buy it outright, but the owners want to consider whether to sell."

"I can't believe it. How ... it's too much. I mean, I was

going to ask you for a loan ... but this?" She flushed and hot tears built up behind her eyes. "I ..." Ava bit down on her lower lip and her voice broke. "I'll pay you back. Draw up a contract and—"

He held up a hand. "I won't hear a word about it."

"You can't just ..." Tears brimmed in her eyes. "This is incredibly sweet but—"

"Ava," he said gently. "It's already done. Think of me as an angel investor. We can discuss terms; if you want to name a cookie after me in return, that would be enough."

She felt heavy and light all at once. Her body didn't know which way was up and she was overcome with a strange wave of dizziness. "I can't believe it."

"Believe it," he murmured. "Because you're going to take this whole world by storm."

She let out a strangled laugh, wiping at the tear on her cheek. "How about we start with just our city and work our way up?"

He slipped his hands around her waist and pulled her against him. "That sounds like a good plan."

Ava tilted her head, studying him. "Why?"

"Why *what*?"

"Why are you being so nice to me? We don't even know if we're going to work out."

He laughed. "Boy, you really know how to ruin a moment, don't you?"

She ducked her head. "Sorry."

Max hooked a finger beneath her chin and lifted it so she was forced to meet his gaze. "Even if we didn't work out, I would still help you because I believe in you." His face lowered closer to hers and his eyes didn't waver. "But I also did it for a bigger reason."

Ava held her breath. He was so close. His proximity was

doing what it always did. Her pulse roared and she went lightheaded.

"I love you, Ava. I have always loved you. From the first moment we met, I knew you would make a mark on my life. I just never imagined that we'd get to this point. You mention us not working out, but I'm here to tell you I'm going to do whatever it takes to ensure we do."

She exhaled a shuddering breath. "Oh."

"I'd like it very much if I could kiss you now."

"Oh," she repeated.

"Is that a yes? No strings attached."

Ava tilted her head slightly. "I don't think I can agree to those terms."

He frowned momentarily.

"If you're going to make all these promises, and ask to kiss me, you better have the capital to back it all up."

His lips curled into a devilish grin. "Well, Ms. Brooks, how about we step into your new office and discuss terms." Max reached for her hand and she held back, causing him to shoot her one more look of confusion. With a tug of her hand, she pulled him toward her.

In one swift motion, she wrapped her hands around his neck, and captured his mouth with her own. This wasn't like any of their other kisses. This one was full of promises, both kept and broken. It was one that told a story of their future, while learning from their past mistakes.

This was a kiss that would be forever remembered as the moment her future changed for the better.

Because now they had each other.

Chapter Twenty-Seven

One year later

Max balanced the stack of red-and-white boxes with one hand as he reached for the door handle that led to the common room at Maple Gardens. The second he entered, his mother came hustling over.

"Oh, good. You have more. I can't tell you how popular these cookies have been with the residents here."

"Oh, I'm aware," Max offered. "I don't think there's a single week that goes by where Ava doesn't mention stopping by to bring you and your little matchmaking group a box."

His mother gave him a knowing smile. "I think you can safely say we earned every single calorie."

Max rolled his eyes good-naturedly. "Alright, alright, I get it. Without your little group none of my friends would have found love."

"And don't you ever forget it." She poked him in the chest. "Now all we're waiting for is the sound of wedding bells."

"Mom," he groaned. "I get that we're in a better place ...

and yes, if it weren't for you I wouldn't have Ava in my life again ... but I don't think I'm ready to tell you every single detail ..." He trailed off when he got a good look at his mother.

She stared at him with her hand on her hip and that look that told him she wasn't having any of his excuses.

He laughed. "Okay, I give. It's tonight. I have it all planned out. We're going to eat at that restaurant we went to with her ex-boyfriend, because she's gonna think it's hilarious, and I want to start making better memories at places like that. Then we're going for a walk down memory lane. You know—that park where there was an outdoor concert. I want her to remember everything good that has happened ... and I'm going to ask her to marry me tonight."

Max blinked a few times and the hairs lifted on his arms. His mother was no longer looking at him. Instead, she was staring over his shoulder at something else.

Or someone else.

Uh oh.

He'd gotten so distracted talking about his plans, he'd completely forgotten that Ava had been chatting with Izzie at the front reception desk.

"She's right behind me, isn't she?"

Lily's eyes darted to meet his, wide and full of amusement. "I'm sorry to say this, dear, but yes. Yes, she is."

Slowly, he turned to face Ava. She face was a blank mask. He couldn't tell if what he'd said was something she wanted or not. And now that he didn't have the upper hand of surprise, he couldn't exactly play it out beforehand to see if she was on board. Had this gone the way he wanted it to, he would have asked her where she saw them in the future.

If she'd brushed off his question, he might have decided to wait. He wanted to read the situation before putting his heart out there.

Now it was too late.

There was no looking back.

All Max could do was offer her a crooked smile. "Hey, Ava."

She blinked.

"You didn't by any chance just walk up, did you? Or perhaps you didn't hear a single word I just said?"

Ava shot a quick look at Lily, then swung her eyes back to Max. "I'm pretty sure we promised we'd never lie to each other." She put the last of the cookie boxes on a nearby table.

Even after all these years of knowing her, he still couldn't get a read on her when she didn't want him to. Ava could be thrilled. She could be secretly jumping up and down just waiting for him to get down on one knee.

Or she might be apprehensive, waiting for him to show his cards so she could turn him down. While he didn't think she would do that—not after the year they'd had together—he wasn't sure she was ready to move forward.

With him.

Max's cheek twitched and he pressed his fingertips there. "Well, you got me. So, what's it gonna be?"

"*What's it gonna be?* Oh no, mister. You're not going to ask me to spend the rest of my life with you that way. Come on! You can do better than that." The corners of her lips quirked upward and that's when he saw it. The humor, the teasing, the Ava he knew and loved.

He sauntered toward her. "Too bad you ruined the surprise. I can't exactly ask you now, can I?"

"Oh, enough with the back and forth, you two!" Lily groaned. "Maximus, will you just ask her already, so the two of you can go on your date to celebrate?"

"What makes you think she's even going to say yes?" he scoffed.

She gave him a flat look then gestured toward Ava. "Look at her. No woman in their right mind would put up with half the stuff she does. I say you better get on that knee of yours before she escapes."

He let out a laugh as he glanced toward the love of his life. "She's got a point, Ava."

Ava stood with her arms crossed. Fingertips tapped on her arm and she smirked at him. "Yeah, I suppose she does."

Max continued moving toward her, grinning like the idiot he was. Then he shoved his hand into his pocket, causing Ava's eyeline to dip toward the movement. Suddenly her eyes went wide and she covered her mouth with her hands.

He laughed at the absurdity. "You're not surprised. Stop acting—"

Ava reached out and whacked his arm with her fingertips. "I didn't think you'd have the ring with you."

"You didn't?"

Her voice dropped to a whisper and she stepped into him, allowing him to slip one arm around her back. "See? You can still surprise me."

The way her hushed voice wrapped around him, holding him to her, was stronger than anything that could physically keep him rooted to this moment.

She snuggled closer to him. "So? Do you have a question for me, or what?"

Lily crooned behind him, Ava snickered, and he rolled his eyes. Max took her hand in his, lifting it to his lips, before he slowly dropped to one knee. His heart hammered, making it incredibly difficult to focus.

"This wasn't how I had imagined it," he murmured.

"This is *exactly* how I imagined it." Ava's eyes shone with delight.

"Will you—"

"Yes."

"I didn't even ask," he laughed. "Or show you the ring."

She pulled him to his feet. "You have been by my side since

before I can remember. I don't need all the fanfare. I don't need a fancy date. I don't even need the likely gorgeous ring you have in your pocket." Her arms wrapped around his neck and she drew closer. "All I need is you."

He couldn't agree more.

Visit Phillipa's website for more book news.

About the Author

Phillipa lives just outside a beautiful town in country Victoria, Australia. She also lives in the many worlds of her imagination and stockpiles stories beside her laptop.

She writes from the heart about love, dreams, secrets, discovery, the sea, the world as she knows it... or wishes it could be. She loves happy endings, heart-pounding suspense, and characters who stay with you long after the final page.

With a passion for music, the ocean, animals, nature, reading, and writing, she is often found in the vegetable garden pondering a new story.

Phillipa's website is www.phillipaclark.com

Also by Phillipa Nefri Clark

Detective Liz Moorland

Lest We Forgive

Lest Bridges Burn

Lest Tides Turn

Connected to this series through several characters is

Last Known Contact

Rivers End Romantic Women's Fiction

The Stationmaster's Cottage

Jasmine Sea

The Secrets of Palmerston House

The Christmas Key

Taming the Wind

Temple River Romantic Women's Fiction

The Cottage at Whisper Lake

The Bookstore at Rivers End

The House at Angel's Beach

Charlotte Dean Mysteries

Christmas Crime in Kingfisher Falls

Book Club Murder in Kingfisher Falls

Cold Case Murder in Kingfisher Falls

Plan to Murder in Kingfisher Falls

Festive Felony in Kingfisher Falls

Daphne Jones Mysteries

Daph on the Beach

Time of Daph

Till Daph Do Us Part

The Shadow of Daph

Tales of Life and Daph

Bindarra Creek Rural Fiction

A Perfect Danger

Tangled by Tinsel

Maple Gardens Matchmakers

The Heart Match

The Christmas Match

The Menu Match

The Cookie Match

Doctor Grok's Peculiar Shop Short Story Collection

Simple Words for Troubled Times
(Short non-fiction happiness and comfort book)

❄